Policies of Exclusion, Poverty and Health:
Stories from the Front

Policies of Exclusion, Poverty and Health:
Stories from the Front

Compiled, Introduction and reports by

Chrystal Ocean

WISE Society, Duncan BC.

Copyright © 2005 by WISE
(Wellbeing through Inclusion Socially & Economically)
www.wise-bc.org
Cover photo © Pamela Sangster

All rights reserved

Printed in Victoria BC by Printorium BookWorks

Library and Archives Canada Cataloguing in Publication

Policies of exclusion, poverty and health : stories from the front / compiled, introduction and reports by Chrystal Ocean.

ISBN 0-9736664-0-4

1. Poor women--British Columbia--Cowichan Valley--Biography.
2. Poor women--British Columbia--Cowichan Valley.
I. Ocean, Chrystal, 1950-
II. WISE Society (B.C.)

HQ1459.B7P64 2005   362.83'086'942097112   C2004-906765-6

Acknowledgements

This project would never have been undertaken without the encouragement and support of Ronnie Phipps, my friend and Coordinator of the BC Coalition for Health Promotion. Ronnie's support was unwavering, despite her many commitments, and was especially strengthened during my bad times. Second only to Ronnie is Agnes Lui, Programs Officer at Status of Women Canada. Both women believed in me when I could not believe in myself.

Aly Stubbs, of the Vancouver Island Providence Community Association, helped Ronnie and I bring the group Wellbeing through Inclusion Socially & Economically (WISE) into existence. Soon after, Bonnie Thompson, Sheila Sanders of the Cowichan Valley Basket Society and Cornelia Wicki of Cowichan Women Against Violence Society joined us. All five women became members of the Board when WISE temporarily established itself as a non-profit Society in April 2004. Around the same time, Pam Clement began adding her enthusiastic encouragement. These wonderful women stayed the course until WISE outgrew the need for their guardianship.

Margaret Hess, of the Canadian Mental Health Association — Cowichan Valley Branch, offered facilities and administrative support. She was also instrumental in the project obtaining additional funding from the Vancouver Foundation. Patti Lusk and Sonya Young, both at the CMHA office, have been particularly helpful and kind.

Beth Stewart contributed her marketing, recruitment and writing skills. Without Beth's efforts early in the project, we may not have enlisted such a fine group of women.

Angela Scotton came onboard originally as one of the storytellers. She has since helped share the load. Her enthusiasm, sensitivity, business acumen, and community relations skills have been a boon to this project and to WISE.

We thank Pamela Sangster for contributing the powerful cover photo. According to Pamela, she was walking down a street in Ireland when she spotted the concrete statue of a nude woman (well, she does have boots on!) standing in front of a closed door. "It spoke volumes."

Not least, we are grateful to our major funders, Status of Women Canada and Vancouver Foundation. Status of Women provided additional help in a contribution toward the cost of printing and binding this book. We note them as sponsors of two of our stories.

Finally, the women for whom this project was proposed, the storytellers, deserve the greatest credit of all. I cannot name them to protect their identity, but they know who they are. Women, you courageously told your stories — and then let them go — because you wanted to make a difference. You ARE making a difference. I cannot adequately express how grateful I am to have met you, how proud I am to know you and how much I admire what you have done.

To every one of you, Thank You.

--Chrystal Ocean

Contents

Acknowledgements v
Introduction 1
The Stories
    Chris 7
    Anna 13
    Brooke 19
    Dana 25
    Elysia 30
    Fallon 36
    Glenna 42
    Halona 48
    India 54
    Jade 60
    Kaelyn 66
    Lucy 72
    Manon 78
    Nancy 84
    Olivia 88
    Paige 94
    Rayna 100
    Sheree 106
    Tatum 112
    Vanessa 118
    Waneta 124
Project Reports
    Phase I – The Issues 133
        Predictors of poverty 135
        Primary effects of poverty 139
        Secondary conditions and their effects 143
        The Future 154
    Phase II – The Recommendations 157
        R1 Awareness and understanding 159
            Mobilize 161
            Galvanize 165
            Politicize 168

Policies of Exclusion, Poverty & Health

The Reports
    Phase II - The Recommendations
        R2 Community-based action...................... 169
            Gift Economy................................. 169
            Moneyless Exchanges.......................... 172
            Co-operatives................................ 173
        R3 Role of government.......................... 174

Introduction

In the summer of 2003, in exasperation with a system that appeared to have no heart a woman named Chris wrote her story of painful marginalization. With the urging of friends, the story came to the attention of an understanding Programs Officer at Status of Women Canada. Together, they convinced Chris to write a proposal for a project. From that beginning, the group Wellbeing through Inclusion Socially and Economically (WISE) was conceived and its project "Policies of Exclusion, Poverty and Health: Stories from the Front" was born.

This book represents the results of that project. It was produced for and by the storytellers themselves, and by Chris, whose real name is Chrystal Ocean.

Funded by Status of Women Canada and the Vancouver Foundation, the project had a twofold purpose: a) to collect stories from women living below Canada's poverty line and b) to provide a vehicle for these women to raise their concerns to the general public and policymakers. Matching that purpose, the project unfolded in two phases. The first involved the difficult yet powerful process of story collection. The second involved the women working together to develop recommendations for the elimination of poverty in Canada. The outcomes of both phases contain surprises, some shocking, some defying contemporary research and expectations.

There were three criteria for eligibility: i) the participant must be female, ii) her household income must fall below Statistics Canada's Low Income Cut Offs (LICOs 2003), and iii) she must live in the Cowichan Valley, a geographical region on Vancouver Island encompassing small urban and rural communities.

I had set an arbitrary figure of 24 as the maximum number of stories to be collected. While this number was obtained, one storyteller was subsequently disqualified, one withdrew and another moved out of province. The remaining 21 stories are included in this book. While the women were given the choice of writing their own stories or having one of two interviewers assist them, I urged the latter, since my own experience suggested that the process might be too painful for them to go through alone.

It was key that the stories and the process do justice to the women and their experiences, and that the stories reveal who these women were in terms of overall values and attitudes. This was about addressing stereotypes and especially about honouring the wishes of my newfound friends. As the project progressed, it became obvious how much these women wanted to see themselves in their stories, not just the facts of their lives in poverty.

All stories except two are 2500 words. All stories are in the first-person and in the women's own words. Participants were not introduced to the others until after their stories were completed. Two stories, including my own, were written by the women themselves. Three stories, having begun by interview, were completed by the participants.

Fifteen of the stories in this book were derived from the transcript of one-on-one meetings between the storyteller and myself. Transcript lengths ranged from 5,000 to 12,000 words. All questions were open-ended. The word 'interview' is used loosely. I would insert questions only if, within the course of a story's unfolding, questions relevant to the project had not been addressed. In the last session, a storyteller was given print copies of her story and the transcript — everything she had said on tape. This allowed comparison between the transcript and the final product. In seven of the 15 cases, portions from sessions done with original interviewer Beth Stewart were included in the final outcome.

When I started doing story interviews, I expected the women would be more distraught during the process than turned out to be the case. Time and again, I heard the words 'validating', 'empowering', and I saw in the women's faces a new pride. As they listened to me read their stories out loud in our final session together, it was clear they felt sadness, but it was also clear they heard their own strength. I am guessing most had not known it was still there. The process proved to be as valuable to the women as the outcome, the story itself.

In keeping with the principle that guided this project from the outset, the two reports included at the end of this book, "Phase 1 — The Issues" and "Phase 2 — The Recommendations," are written in the first-person plural.

The stories in this collection are unedited, but for changes to protect the women's identity or to prevent the identity of for-profit enterprises that do not offer government-funded programs. For example, dates, some geographical names, and the names of department or grocery stores are withheld, while the names of non-

Introduction

governmental organizations (NGOs) engaged in relevant government-funded programs — sometimes referred to as partner programs — are not.

Two additional NGOs are mentioned in the stories: the Salvation Army (also known as 'the Sally Ann') and WAVAW (Women Against Violence Against Women). WAVAW is the only organization in the Cowichan Valley offering counselling and other services specifically geared to women and families who have experienced violence. Any attempt to hide its identity would be pointless and also unnecessary.

When a storyteller talks of 'the food bank' or 'soup kitchen', she almost always means the organization closest to her home that provides food services to low-income people. There are one or more food banks in most locales in the Cowichan Valley.

The report, "Phase 1 — The Issues," represents my own interpretation and analysis, supported by the storytellers, of the dominant themes in our stories. The report, "Phase 2 — The Recommendations," details the recommendations developed by the storytellers for both policy change and the personal actions other women in poverty might take to help eradicate poverty in their communities.

The stories present the reality of these women's lives in their own words and as they see it. While neither WISE nor I take a position regarding the validiity of their statements, we wholeheartedly support these women's right to have their voices heard.

The method by which a story was created is indicated in the following manner:

Auto indicates a story written by the woman herself.

Auto to Interview is a story that began as auto, but was completed by interview.

Interview indicates a story constructed by the interviewer from the storyteller's own words, taken from transcript.

Interview to Auto is a story that began by interview but was completed by the storyteller.

All finalized stories required the storytellers' signed approval regardless of method used.

The Stories

Chris[1]

Method: Auto

Sponsored by: Status of Women Canada

I have written my story with the hope that somewhere, sometime a policymaker will read it and come to see that government employment and financial assistance programs effectively marginalize the mentally ill. I hope further that it will be seen that poverty not only can cause mental illness, but that it feeds mental illness, helping it to flourish.

I recognize now that my mental illness began when I was 4, manifested in a feeling of deep despair, felt physically as a permanent lump in my throat and tension in my abdomen.

At 4, I had come to know that, to the extent that my mother thought of me at all, it was in terms of how I would serve her. Essentially, she aimed to shape me into an object that exemplified her view of herself, that of a being of the utmost perfection, beauty, and intelligence whose very presence bestowed a blessing upon others. This object of her creation was expected to adore her, to exhibit no human frailties, to be invisible unless called upon to serve, to be quiescent, to have no will (and so no identity) of its own.

My sibling, one year younger than me, was viewed as less malleable. That he was a boy didn't help. Our mother gave him up early, when he was 3, to the first couple that would take him. This was the second and final time my brother and I were separated.

I dared to beg in the early years that my mother give me up too but she didn't — until I was almost 14 and then it was to the Toronto Children's Aid Society (CAS). After my brother left, I missed him of course, but was relieved that he had escaped early before, I naively assumed, any damage had been done.

Once I was handed over to the CAS, it took four months before I noticed that the children being placed in foster homes were the children who were cutting themselves. Suffice it to say that soon after I was placed in a foster home too. By Christmas of that year,

---

[1] This story originated the project. See introduction.

however, I realized something else, that I didn't know how to receive or give affection. The guilt drove me to attempt suicide.

Since suicide was a criminal offence in those days, I was brought before a judge and sentenced to Toronto's Lakeshore Psychiatric Hospital (LPH). At 14 I was the youngest patient they'd had and they didn't know what to do with me.

One month after I arrived at LPH, my CAS worker told me I had been cleared to leave the hospital. This surprised me, since I had seen a psychiatrist twice and felt no better than on my arrival. My worker also told me that the CAS couldn't find a foster home for me and that I would have to stay at LPH until something came up. This turned out to be ten months later.

Psychiatric Visits: Within a week of arriving at LPH, I was seen briefly by a psychiatrist who assessed me as 'emotionally disturbed'. A month later, I was seen even more briefly by another psychiatrist. The third and last visit was eleven months after my arrival, its purpose being to formalize my release.

Life at LPH: LPH housed people whose mental health ranged widely, from the perfectly normal to the criminally insane. Among the patients was i) a 15-year-old male who was there for monitoring the drug therapy for his epilepsy, ii) a 16-year-old female who kept cutting herself, iii) a woman in her mid-40s who stopped screaming only when she slept, iv) a 26-year-old male who sought to kill police officers whenever he drank a drop of beer.

The last of these, Bruce, became my best friend. In fact, he was my first love. Although it would have been easy for Bruce to take advantage of me, we were always and to the end constant companions only. I trusted him and he never hurt me.

I witnessed horrible things at LPH, including shock treatments, and I came to know and become friends with many twisted, not-so-twisted, normal and merely eccentric people. LPH felt like home to me. It still does. I pine for that sense of belonging, community, and acceptance that I felt when I was there. In all other situations and places, I feel awkward and an outsider and don't know how to interact with people.

A couple of months into my stay at LPH, I was given a battery of tests to determine my IQ and vocational aptitude. Although I was discovered to have a genius IQ, the CAS sent me to secretarial school. Being a secretary, apparently, was the height to which a female could aspire in the 60s.

After LPH, my life, with depression always lurking, soared and plunged its weary way. I was gang raped at 15 with more sexual

Chris

bandying-about to follow, married and divorced twice, and raised two children. The life of wife and mother doesn't feel like mine, although this body bears the scars of pregnancy and childbirth.

Intellectually curious, I began to pursue learning opportunities in my 30s. I studied high school calculus and physics via distance education. At 41, I began university study, the first dozen courses also by distance education. At 43, I switched to on-campus study and by 45, had finished my BA and MA. I won awards and scholarships, including the SSHRC for doctoral studies, and got within months of completing a double PhD.

Throughout my doctoral studies, the depression gave me few breaks and I felt a building tension. The life and identity I was trying to discover or create was beginning to unravel. I've tried to understand why and suspect that it's because the postgraduate process is another form of indoctrination, of learning to think and do in a prescribed way as dictated by others. Oddly, this indoctrination is more pronounced the higher one goes up the academic ladder. Where you might expect more freedom for creativity and inventiveness to flourish, you find instead added restrictions. Further, the very nature of academic study involves argument, with students expected to 'assert' a thesis or 'defend' a position. Things are much more a battleground than a playground.

All my life I've avoided battlegrounds. In the summer of 2000 I abandoned my efforts for the doctorate and came home to BC. I still had an MA, had always been able to find work and had entrepreneurial instincts. I've been a stenographer, bookkeeper, go-go dancer, letter carrier, pizza delivery driver, choreographer, dance instructor, computer consultant, web designer, census representative, elections officer, university instructor, conference presenter, small business owner. I've lost track of the number of things I've done and the skills I've learned, most self-taught. It never occurred to me that I'd be unable to find work.

Having been a student for the previous seven years, I had very little money, but what I did have, in the form of a small RRSP, I put into an old mobile home and a down payment on a new car. My intention had been to buy a ten-year-old Toyota, not a new car, but no one would approve a loan for this. It turns out that if you're out of the country for a period of time (I'd been studying the PhD elsewhere), your credit record is wiped clean. Same with your driving record. At 50, I had to start all over again, rebuilding my credit and paying the maximum in car insurance.

Policies of Exclusion, Poverty & Health

There was nothing left with which to furnish the mobile and it remained as it was when I moved in: virtually empty and certainly bare. There was no money to buy pots and pans and other kitchen utensils, garden tools and supplies, drapes, paint, sufficient fuel for the winter, a proper bed and chair, and so on. Despite this, the first couple of months I was optimistic. I only became anxious as the weeks, months, and now years, went by.

Early in 2001, into this already stressful situation came a voice from the past. An email from my brother said that he wanted to re-establish our relationship, something I'd yearned for most of my life. However, his contacting me at that time was more than I could handle. He wanted to know all about me, my interests, hopes, attitudes and values. He hoped, he said, that "by learning about you, I will learn about myself." My brother's contact precipitated a downward spiral that continues to this day, aided and abetted by poverty.

I am someone who lives with mental illness daily and is unable to access medical, employment and financial help for reasons that include the mental illness itself.

On the financial front, I don't meet the criteria for government programs. Although in 2000 I was a postgraduate, I wasn't under 30 and therefore wasn't eligible for student programs. Although I'm unemployed, I'm not eligible for EI since I haven't been able to find enough employment to build up the requisite number of hours. Although my income is only $200 a month gross from self-employment, I don't qualify for Welfare since I sold my old mobile home and currently have more than $500 in the bank.

Regarding employment assistance, although I want to find work I'm not eligible for government employment assistance programs, such as JobWave and Community Futures, since I'm not collecting financial assistance. Even if I did qualify for self-employment assistance from Community Futures, the small business I've worked so hard over the past two years to build would not qualify; only NEW self-employment opportunities are funded. Although I'd be happy to get my computer qualifications certified, I'm not eligible for government training assistance programs, again because I'm not collecting financial assistance.

My new car was repossessed — by that time I'd have owned an old Toyota. My chances of finding employment are even less than before. The one good temporary job I found in 2001 was for Census Canada. A requirement for that job was a car. Ironically I made *just*

Chris

enough with that job to pay my insurance and car payments for the year.

Desperate and within a month of homelessness, in October 2002 I got an offer on my mobile home, which had been up for sale for almost a year. I guiltily bought a decent bed, desk, and desk chair, and bits and pieces like a toilet bowl brush. Most importantly, I used $2000 for advertising, which I knew wouldn't be enough but I had to try. As I write this, there is $5000 left and I continue to live without items that most people take for granted.

I don't go to the doctor, even when something occurs that would have other people making an appointment immediately. There is no point. I don't have the $10/visit fee for physiotherapy to correct my shoulder and back problems, or the $100/year for prescription medication, or the $300+ to be fitted and supplied with orthotics to correct my gait, or ...

I haven't seen a dentist in years. One tooth was chipped three years ago and bites into my cheek, my gums are receding, some teeth are loose. I chew my food carefully to preserve what teeth I have left.

As the poverty increases and I can't find work, my mental health worsens. As my mental health worsens, social interaction becomes harder and I do less well in interviews. I've stopped trying to find an employer, since the repeated rejection has become more than I can bear. I avoid people for fear I'll start crying.

Whatever caused the crisis, I've been unable to get help. Part of the problem is the inability to ask for it. An early and frequent lesson was that help, even a small favour, came only with a price. I also fear that people won't hear me, or if they do they will respond with disdain. The inability to ask for help is so extreme that when I've tried over the past few years by telephone or in person, I panic and freeze into a sort of catatonic state, particularly when someone asks a question with YOU or YOUR in it, words that I hear as accusations.

My financial position encourages an attitude that I've had for as long as I can remember, that of waiting for death. I'm not suicidal in the usual sense, of someone who would take an overt act to end their life. Rather, there is an absence or quashing of the instinct for self-preservation. For example, I suspect I've had two mild heart attacks in the past months. The last time, all I could think of was the state of the corpse and how it might offend the medics who found it. That prompted me to get out of bed, wash up and get dressed, while the tightening in my chest persisted.

I've tried to reach out to the local Mental Health unit, but each time the response has shown a lack of understanding of how crippling mental illness can be. In one phone call, the mental health professional asked, 'What do you want to do?' I told her I couldn't decide, that making decisions became harder the more stressed I became. She just waited at the other end of the line, repeating her question. I hung up and haven't called again.

I've been told of a psychologist who has a private practice in Victoria, one who specializes in abuse of the sort I experienced. His technique sounds like it could help me. I cannot afford him of course, nor the cost of getting there. I am getting some counselling at the local branch of Women Against Violence Against Women (WAVAW). Of all the professionals who have tested and prodded me, from the CAS and LPH to the local Mental Health unit, this counsellor is the only one who has shown empathy. The others have taken notes and distantly observed, as though I were a subject in a lab. It's like talking to a wall.

While I live with mental illness, there is a lot I could contribute to my community and to the cause of the poor and mentally ill. I am particularly passionate about the links between the two and have written to my MP on more than one occasion. Unfortunately and predictably, the responses referred me to the very programs whose eligibility criteria I wrote as excluding people like me. I suspect my letters were never read.

I need to work, not the least because working gives me reason to keep going. I can't feel good about myself for my own sake, but I can, when given the opportunity, feel good about myself for the sake of what I might do for others.

Anna

Method: Interview

Sponsored by: Status of Women Canada

I decided to get involved in this project because I need to be realistic, honest and open about my own struggles with poverty. I was born and raised in poverty. I was affected by poverty. I'm still living in poverty. Being involved with WISE is to help me deal with that realization and to admit that I am also one of those many women out there who are affected by poverty. It is a tough admission. It is. It bothers me as a person who advocates for equality and equal rights and equal opportunity.

I was born in St. Lucia, into the poverty created as a result of colonization. I lived in a segregated part of the Island. In the 70's, my family struggled just to put food on the table. We had no running water, no electricity and no ready-made appliances such as a cooking stove.

At 8 years old I had to fend for myself. I dug the soil for yams, fetched water, hand washed my clothes at the river and cooked my own meals over the open flame. With my mother working day and night, we saw little of each other. She was gone by the time I rose and I was asleep by the time she got home.

By 11 years old I was working to help my family cultivate bananas, attending school three days a week – without the required textbooks –, fishing in the ocean and going to church. These hardships secured us a better lifestyle: a three-bedroom home, running water, electricity, appliances, some clothing, and one or two pairs of shoes. There were still sacrifices. If my shoes were damaged, I walked for miles barefoot. While I had fun moments, my life was exhausting.

By 12 years old I knew that my mother could not ensure me a better future. All she dreamed and hoped for herself, as well as for me, was to be a good Christian. In spite of the lack of financial stability and future security, faithfully and religiously she donated money to the Church. In my opinion, her oppressing belief system deprived me of a stable environment. This realization shaped my determination for economic, social, and educational success. I did not want to remain deprived and uneducated.

Policies of Exclusion, Poverty & Health

The idea of moving to Canada came about when I met ___, a Canadian-born woman with a St. Lucian mother. During her stay in St. Lucia, ___ needed childcare for her two young children. Our deal was that I would live and work with her. Upon her trip back to Canada two years later, she would sponsor me and provide me with a free plane ticket. In the meantime, she would give me an allowance and enrol me into night school, which she would pay for. My Aunty ___ thought this would be a good opportunity. I agreed. At 13 years old I dropped out of elementary school and moved in with ___.

Two years came and went. I never saw inside a classroom. I never got any allowance. On the few occasions I visited my family, I brought the children with me. The younger child called me mummy because he thought I was really his mother. I had a strong bond with them, so for the children's sake as well as my own I remained hopeful. I wanted to believe that I really was going to get a plane ticket from Canada after ___ returned home.

After they left for Canada, I was still waiting for the plane ticket. As a result, I decided to make my own way. I worked in a grocery store and saved some money, but to come up with $1800 for the plane ticket was nearly impossible. To make this trip a reality, my family leant me the little money they had. I applied for my first passport and a few weeks later, I left on a jet plane for Canada.

Before I left my country, it was arranged that ___ would meet me at the airport in Toronto. Indeed, travelling for the first time was very scary. I was afraid that Canadian Immigration would not permit me entry and I was not convinced that ___ would keep her word.

___ did meet me at the airport. After all, she was going to benefit because I would be her free babysitter. In exchange, she would take full responsibilities for me. On our way from the airport, she asked me to pay for the taxi cab.

———

During my first three months in Canada, I lived in a two-bedroom apartment with ___, her mother, sister, and the two children. We were fed and supported by her mother's small income. ___ had no job but was never around to help with the household tasks. By December of that year, ___'s mother was growing impatient, ___ had reconciled with her husband and was moving to Windsor and I was going to be sent back to St. Lucia.

At 15, I thought that choosing to live in Canada was simply a matter of choice. Accordingly, I chose Canada and stayed.

Anna

I was an illegal alien living underground for almost eight years. Until I became a Landed Immigrant, I had no rights. I was not eligible to go to school, engage in employment, get health coverage, receive financial assistance or live in decent housing. I even had to create a false identity. I had to work for little if any pay. For example, immediately after I left the situation with ___, I lived with a Trinidadian family in Toronto. I would do babysitting and housekeeping in exchange for room and board. I was exploited, used, recycled and used some more.

Becoming a Landed Immigrant was a dream come true. Finally freedom, I thought. I got my high school diploma, did a one-year nursing program and worked four years in the nursing field. In September 2000, my children and I moved to BC.

―――

Born and raised in the Caribbean, I can identify with the poverty Haiti goes through. I didn't have to go into the garbage dumps and scramble for food. I was able to go to the banana tree and cut a bunch of bananas, or dig the soil and get yams, or pick a fresh mango from the tree. But pain is pain. If our lives are threatened, from living out of the dumpster or from having to stand on the streets of Vancouver to do prostitution, that's still pain. The difference with North America is that poverty is hidden. We can live in an apartment and in a house or in a setting where we can mask that poverty. People really don't take the time to get to know you, to know how you're struggling. People in the community, they've stopped supporting each other and the village no longer raises the child.

The student loans are not enough even to pay the rent — which this month I scrambled every single penny to pay. There was nothing left, not even for cat food. For two days, the cats were meowing at me. Yesterday I got a cheque in the mail from GST. My family and I literally kissed that cheque, because it meant we could have some groceries. It's just unbelievable.

We have a little bit of land space. We cut the grass and rototill the land. We have a nice little square area where we grow vegetables. It's all in a bush because there's not enough space for everything to grow. For the 15 years of my life in Canada, this is the first time that I have owned a garden. I am very much enjoying it because it reminds me of how I was raised. It was natural for every family member to have their own little patch of land, to grow their own fruits and vegetables.

Here, people without gardens must go to grocery stores. That's how the corporations have taken over. It used to be that people would make cherry pies or vegetable dishes or whatever. They were able to sell that to the neighbours and they would survive that way. Now there are all types of liability issues and insurance and licensing and... When you look at all these big manufacturers, what are they doing but making that very same pie and earning millions and billions in revenue and profit? They've managed to take away the very essence of life in terms of how we survive, and turned it into a multi-billion dollar business. The pie that we get at the grocery store now is less nutritious and has no value and no meaning. In fact, we cannot afford the pie anymore.

I started a business two years ago. To me, being in business is about stability, security, knowing that I will have enough money to someday own my own home, being able to drive a stable vehicle and to put clothes on my children's backs, to feed them. A solid-based profitable business will give me enough financial stability and some type of power where I can influence my life and the lives of other people around me.

I am at the point where I'm realizing that conducting business in North American society is very much different from the society I was born and raised in. If we want to start a business in my country, you get your supplies and whatever else and you're able to set up, you're able to start selling and people will support you. When it comes to the liabilities and legalities of it, we don't have to worry about putting $20,000 – $30,000 into starting a business. We don't have to worry about all this liability insurance, these permits, that licensing. We don't have to worry about how the competition will react or is doing better, or how we need to select our target market group, or do adequate promotions and marketing and sales and advertisement strategies. We don't have to worry about writing 25- to 30-page business plans, financials. All this nonsense is basically another way to oppress people.

By the time you've acquired all those licences and other added expenses, you're looking at $30,000 to $40,000, just to get a small business off the ground; and there's no guarantee that you'll make back your return in even a year. In my society, you can start a business with $500 – $1000 and get a return on investment right away.

Anna

Having been raised in poverty, I do not have $30,000 or $40,000, but unless you have $20,000 or $30,000 in owner's equity or some type of asset, you basically cannot get a loan.

In classes — for example, a FutureCorp program — where we would be getting our financial plans and our business plans done, I've sat beside people whose parents have loaned them $20,000 or $30,000. They're able to be in business the next day. I have struggled to do the market research, to test the market, to introduce the product line to show that it's a viable business concept, to determine that there is a market niche for my products and services, to put in my own money to promote and market my business and to take an advanced business management program. I've gone all those extra steps and I'm still hearing the same thing. Because I don't have assets or equity, I cannot be eligible for a traditional loan. What to do now?

I was speaking with one of the agencies that loans money to small businesses and entrepreneurs. I said, I have done everything that you've asked me to do in terms of the hoops I have to jump through and you're still telling me that I'm not eligible for funding. If I were a Caucasian woman who walked in here with $30,000, with no business background, with no business management skills, would I be getting the money for my business? Yes. I asked, Are there anymore resources that may be of help to me? I was referred to the Disability Resource Centre.

Now with the DRC, I have to prove that I have a disability. It means I have to revisit my past. I have to go back ten years into my life and dredge up some kind of traumatic stress syndrome to be qualified for some type of disability. They are sending a 5-page form to my family doctor to confirm that I have a disability. That's a violation of my human rights, having to play a victim role. I shouldn't be put in the position of having to revisit any illness from 10-15 years ago and show how it still affects me today. Whether or not it does, it shouldn't be a basis and foundation for me getting funding.

Then, they're not prepared to tell me how long the process will take nor am I guaranteed funding by going through all these hoops. Also, when it boils down to it, it's one community agency in the Valley that is making the decisions — whether it be for traditional loans or for disability loans or any type of entrepreneurial loans. That's FutureCorp.

On top of that, if and when I were to get into the program, I would still have to once again go through all the criteria: six or seven steps. I've done all of that: market research, surveys, business plan, financials, promotions... I am already at the final step. I have a business management diploma. So *why should they force me to do the seven steps over again, to retrain?*

When I first got involved in FutureCorp, the first program I did with them cost me $1500. I had to pay for it. With a lot of these programs, if you're not in the system you're not eligible. If you're not a Welfare recipient, you can't get in. If you're not on EI, you can't get in. No matter which way you go, you're blocked. It's unnecessary hardship. It's unnecessary hassle. The very same agencies that are there to help people are in fact oppressing people by making them go through one hoop after another. It's like going through a maze. You enter. You go in one way. Before you know it, you're lost and you can't get out. A lot of these people are not able to think outside of the box nor does the system encourage them to do so.

―――

Our cat adopted us. This cat lived in my complex where I lived before and that cat walked around for months unfed and unkept. Everyone else assumed that the cat was kept by someone else, that it belonged to someone else.

That's the same attitude towards the community. That's the same mentality of us living next door to people and we don't know who they are. We treat them like animals, assuming that they are fed and kept and cared for and that they have a family to belong to. Although poor, I take pride and dignity in taking care of my animals, my family and my community.

Brooke

Method: Interview

My life's complicated. I want my life to be simple, peaceful. How do you get peace and simplicity when you're in really bad poverty? I am vulnerable because of poverty. You run into people who know you're vulnerable and they're bullies.

I was very capable, but at home I didn't get the kind of encouragement that I needed. Mom worked part time in a department store in Montreal and Dad was in the Air Force, so we moved all the time. That's what I remember the most: moving, moving, moving. Also, both my parents were excessive drinkers.

The only time I felt any happiness was when I began working with horses at age 10. I had four girlfriends then and for five years, I had happiness.

My dad was posted primarily to places in Quebec. My dad's best posting was to Comox. In my later teens, I lived in Courtenay. My father had suppressed my character so I was introverted and quiet. I befriended the wildest girl in school, so it was like night and day walking together. With her, life was never boring; there was always action. I loved dancing and I liked music. It always bothered me that I didn't get my Grade 12. I'd still like to do that, when my life settles down.

I had a boy when I was 20 and had my daughter when I was 28. I would like to be closer. It makes me sad that they don't have the heart that they would like to help me, although I don't expect them to.

I was 25 when I got married. If I had to do it over again, I wouldn't have married him. Because of my dysfunctional family, I didn't have the tools to make the right decision. He was a drinker and it got worse as the years went on. We had a hobby farm in Sahtlam and I really enjoyed that. I got my first horse at 33.

When my ex walked out, I said, thank you for a second chance; but losing the hobby farm is a part of my life that is very heart wrenching. Looking back, I didn't get enough money for it.

I bought a log house (it used to be a honey shack) and I converted it to up and down bedrooms. I had always thought that the family should work together – my mother and my family were all there – so we did that. We all pitched in together. But what I didn't know was that I was the only one with that thought, and one day my mother said that she was leaving. She knew that I couldn't manage on my own. Then my son decided to go with her, because he wouldn't have to pay any rent. So my family abandoned me and I lost my home.

That was a very tough period. That's when the feeling of poverty really hit me.

———

For so long, it has been difficult to go and get groceries, something which other people take for granted. Poverty keeps people away. It excludes me socially. I don't have a car on the road or have a phone. I can't entertain. I have had to be in survival mode for over ten years. I've moved a lot too. You can't get a decent place to live, and right now I have to move again because people are drinking and drugging and stealing and running around all hours of the night. Your home should be a sanctuary.

Recently my income has been zero. The reason I have been able to get by with no money for the past two years is that I connected with a man who pretended he was my friend. He allowed me to stay in his house.

Six months ago, I was homeless. My 'friend' used to help me out somewhat and then he left town. He used to take me out once in a while for lunch. This was a platonic friend. Three years. To me, he was like a brother. So he found himself a girlfriend; and I was out, my stuff was out, the house was put up for sale.

I had a small garage sale, but that doesn't bring a lot of money. All I could think about was finding work.

I did a work exchange [after that]. I was able to stay in this old house and I did yard work and cleaning. This person knew that I was struggling, so they offered me a place to live until I got on my feet. They would take me out to lunch once in a while.

I shared with you that I was homeless with this man friend. Well six months after that, I was homeless again. And, *ohhh*, I didn't think that would happen to me twice in six months! I met a real estate lady and she decided that I should meet these people that bought a farm south of town and I could work on this farm with this family. So I met them and it seemed OK at first. We had a plan and it was supposed to be done by September. Come September and the plan did not go through. I did work for the family and with no income. Her

Brooke

partner had cancer, so she decided to put the farm up for sale. It was gone in a week. Then she asked me to leave the residence. She gave me very little time. I was homeless *again*.

I decided I should go back into Transition House, where women can stay who have been abused. It's a large comfortable home, and the FOOD ... I was comfortable in the Transition House.... I'm *so tired* of my needs not being met. I'm *so tired* of moving all the time. I felt good there, I felt comfortable, I would have liked to stay there until I had work.

They just don't allow it. I don't fit. Sometimes I just feel like I don't fit anywhere.

There's never been enough food. I'm always searching for food. The Church gives small food vouchers. Friends, the odd time, will feel led to give me money for food. The odd time, I get invited to supper. I like to eat healthy: fruits, vegetables, good yogurt, grain cereal, smoked salmon. Didn't know that the poor weren't supposed to have a preference!

I am thankful we have a Food Bank and so on, but it just is not enough. I've gone to the Sally Ann but they only give me food three times a year. What I am talking about is two bags of groceries. Every day they do put out bread and a few things, but only in the morning. I go to the Food Bank once a month. I buy a lot of bananas. I have a sweet tooth and I eat dates for that.

Not having a car and not having a phone are big barriers, as is being an older woman.

Regarding public financial assistance, most of the time I didn't try because I wanted to remain independent. They make you jump through hoops. That is the hard part. It is overwhelming. I look through the papers and all the rents are at least $500, then you have to try to find a way to eat too. I think they should allow you to work part time to get enough food.

I had been on social assistance before, a few years ago. You don't get it right away. It takes three weeks before you get the money. You have to make an appointment three weeks before, and then they still may say 'no' to you. I could go there in need and still have to wait.

Getting assistance is not: 'Oh I've got income, now I'm OK'.

It doesn't work like that. For me, it was hard with them. I needed more help than I was getting, and then they want to know a lot about your personal life and what you're doing. They thought that I was this man's girlfriend. And another time, I rented this basement suite and they thought that the man who was upstairs ... *I was not his girlfriend*. And they wouldn't give me money. Then I was at Horizons [a pre-employment program], and they went over on my behalf and said: "Look, this woman is in need." Then it was OK, for a short time.

Because of this man friend, I got an RV to have somewhere to sleep, somewhere to live. I wanted to do it all on my own, but I couldn't. With renting, there always seems to be issues. 'Could you reduce the rent by even $50?' They wouldn't. I was moving all the time. But then I got trouble when I had the RV. People misunderstood what was going on and why I had a second hand RV. So I had to keep moving the RV and that got to be too stressful. So I put it up for sale.

I was on assistance at that time. This one woman, a new worker, she came up with – you know, the woman who investigates; with Welfare, they come up to the house and investigate you? – well, there was that woman. This other young woman and the worker came up and both saw my RV - I would gladly give them the RV for their home. The new worker went out of her way to make sure that I would lose my RV. She said: This is not shelter. So I looked up the word *shelter*: "a place out of the wind and the rain." They wanted to make my life more difficult, cut back on my money. It got so bad ... and this girl was *pleased* with herself that she had made my life harder. It's another thing to be nasty, but she was pleased that she did me that harm.

That's when I walked away from assistance.

———

I got ill last year because of stress, which is a killer. I got so tired of being poor. I found it so stressful that I wanted to die. The doctor said I wouldn't get better, but I did.

I had an overactive thyroid problem. My eyes were bulgy and I got real skinny. I kept going down and down. I was not able to eat the way I wanted to. Actually, in the Bible it was the poor man's diet. Now it's the rich man's diet. I had to be creative in getting the money for the pills. A friend did buy me some. Twice a year I have to go and get checked up at the lab. My illness did affect me when I was sick [with stress]. But I decided I didn't want to be sick anymore and I am much better now. My thyroid condition doesn't prevent me from doing things now.

Where I live is too small. I have a TV, a loveseat and a vanity. I sleep on a baby's mattress. Heat is included. There is a tiny bathroom.

Brooke

I don't stay home all the time. I get out. But I need to connect with more people. I don't have enough friends. I would like to have a close female and male friend.

I have used the bus but find it is not scheduled for the working person. You have to have $1.25 every time, so I walk a lot — or I bike or get a ride. It is hard to do things because I have to get a ride to do them.

It is very hard. My parents are gone; my kids are doing their own thing. My relationship with my daughter is slowly getting better. I wish she would grasp the fact that I am getting older though. My relationship with my son is not good. He is fearful I will ask for something.

I used to have pets, but not now because I need to be settled. I had Cooper, an orange male cat. I got him as a baby. I miss him.

I find treasures in the darkness. My spirituality does really help me have a different perspective on the dark times. One of my treasures ... is that I never take anything for granted; I have compassion for the poor and I like simple things. For example, if someone invites me to dinner, it is very special. I enjoy food very much.

I am really interested in photography and horses. In fact, I like all animals. I'd like to go to live theatre and I'd like to do some modelling. I like being creative — and I like things of character, like older homes and older cars. I have written some poetry.

I'd like to be employed. I am taking pictures in order to become established as a professional photographer. I was so disappointed when Queen Margaret's wouldn't hire me. I knew I could be a benefit to them.

One of the main barriers to finding work is not having a vehicle. The only other way would be to get a friend to drive me until I could get on my feet. I have a lot of experience working with horses and would be a real benefit to someone.

I need a phone for work. I need car insurance, even if it is just for six months. A car. I say, Help me so I can help myself. It would help me if once in a while I could have some $50 food certificates so I could meet my basic needs. Also I need help with getting good second hand clothes so I could be presentable for work.

I still have hope. Where would you be without hope? I still have hope for the future. One thing I want to do is make more connections with people. You need connections to find work and the right place to live.

Policies of Exclusion, Poverty & Health

Poverty sucks! I am not depressed, I am deprived. I am in despair and I am frustrated. Before, the poverty hurt so bad that I wanted to go to sleep and never wake up. But now I want to be of help to other people. I have learned so much. At the church that I go to, there's a special fund that you can give to, which I do for people in need. And I give specifically for that purpose.

Dana

Method: Interview to auto

The difficulties of my life began even before I was born.

My mom was raised by a passive father and a mother who was overly domineering, critical and controlling. As a result of the emotional abuse she endured as a child she suffered a nervous breakdown when she was 18. She spent a very scary month in the psychiatric unit of Vancouver General Hospital. During her committal, a relationship formed between her and Father, also a patient at the time. He was an alcoholic who had been admitted to sober up. When released, Mom, who could not bear the thought of returning home to her parents, ran away with my dad instead.

I was born in Abbotsford, B.C. My first birthday was marked by the arrival of my brother, my second birthday by the arrival of my sister. By age 3, I was an overly self-sufficient and helpful toddler. After years of being subjected to the alcoholic abuse of her husband, Mom finally got the courage to leave him after he assaulted her. On her own with three babies, she returned to her parents for help.

I was raised by three parents: a chronically depressed mother, an emotionally abusive grandmother and a passive grandfather. Hardship, poverty and fear of the future defined my childhood. Grandma continued to treat Mom poorly and focused her attention on all my faults, the biggest one being I reminded her of Mom.

We moved frequently due to economic changes in Mom's life and the coming and going of three different stepfathers. I attended four different schools by Grade 5. Grandma babysat us before and after school and at school breaks.

We moved to Lake Cowichan partway through Grade 6. After a year there, stepfather number three left. I was 14 years old and felt abandoned and rejected by four fathers. When we moved from the city of Abbotsford to the small community of Lake Cowichan, I went through culture shock. For a variety of reasons I never fit in with my peers, primarily because I did not know how to be a kid. I was Mom's main support person, the one she relied on for help with household chores. By age 12, I did most of the cooking for my family. Eventually she forgot that I was just a kid and expected me to act like a mini-adult.

Policies of Exclusion, Poverty & Health

I started working part-time just before my 16th birthday. Most of my earnings went into the family unit. It never occurred to me to save for my education because the family's need was greater.

I was bored all through high school, yet maintained straight A's. Starting in Grade 11, I took all university transferable courses. Then I realized there was no money for my post secondary education. After that I started having panic attacks as I approached school. Feeling sick all the time, I was repeatedly tested for mono but every test was negative. I was depressed and worn out from too much adult responsibility. Feeling ostracized by the kids at school, I quit.

At 16, I fell for the advances of a 25-year-old man who was introduced to me by Mom. He seemed to be the only one who wanted me. I was living with him and pregnant by the time I was 17. He was even more critical, controlling and angry than Grandma was. I enrolled in upgrading courses that were repeatedly interrupted due to my partner's behaviour. I finally had the courage to leave him six months after my second baby was born.

By 21, I was a single parent on Welfare. My only job history was working in restaurants on both sides of the grill. Freed from constant problems of my relationship, I continued to work part-time while completing Grades 11 and 12.

I wanted to be a high school Math and Science teacher. I was too afraid of the large student loan debt I'd need to incur. Even with an education, Mom couldn't make enough money to get completely off Welfare or to make her student loan payments.

Instead I took a ten-month Accounting course at Malaspina.[2] I completed my course with top marks and moved to Victoria to find employment. I had no idea how to present myself professionally and could not secure employment in the accounting field. I returned to waitressing at a busy restaurant and discovered that with the combination of wages and tips, I could make far better money than in an accounting position. I worked there for five years. I loved it and was very good at it. I stepped into the Manager's position while she was on maternity leave. I had job security, job satisfaction, medical, dental and prescription benefits. I had established my credit and had saved $14,000 for a down payment on a house. I finally believed that life could be good.

In 1997 that all changed. Early that year I was rear-ended by a young driver. Off work for three months, by the Fall I was back working full-time. A month later, I was assaulted by my live-in

---

[2] A local college-university.

Dana

boyfriend. I left him and moved into a new place. Before the year was out, I was again involved in an accident. Another young driver drove into the back of my truck, forcing me into the vehicle in front. My injuries were extensive enough to end my waitressing days. I was also diagnosed with Post Traumatic Stress Disorder. I have been battling chronic pain and depression ever since. Initially ICBC compensated me for my lost wages but that didn't last long. After I'd exhausted my house savings and UIC, I applied for Income Assistance benefits.

The first year following the second accident was a very bleak time. To lose everything I'd worked for was almost more than I could bear. I was unable to care for my children properly and they continued to live with their dad in the Cowichan Valley.

Shortly after my second accident, my ex-boyfriend returned, wanting to get back together. I dated him for a brief period and then broke it off for good. Two weeks later I discovered that I was pregnant. In many ways, this baby saved me. He was the motivation for me to try to return to the land of the living. Immediately after he was born, I moved back to the Cowichan Valley, feeling the need to reconnect with my two older children. They spent their time equally between both homes.

After three years of physical rehab, I worked in two jobs in the fitness field. ICBC settled a year after I had returned to work. Most of that money went to paying off the debt I'd incurred while being unemployed. A year and a half ago, I lost my full-time job, but was able to retain my minimal part-time job. I therefore had to re-apply for Income Assistance.

In April 2002, when the Ministry changes went through, they cut my support by $417, the biggest part being the loss of the $200 earnings exemption. Six weeks after receiving that news, my little son was diagnosed with Duchenne's Muscular Dystrophy, which is an incurable condition that reduces his life expectancy. I suddenly found myself needing additional support at a time when resources were being cut. Those cuts created a bigger gap in the safety net and we fell through it.

I applied for the Disability Tax Benefit of $130/month. I was turned down. My son isn't 'sick enough' yet. I applied for the Fuel Tax Number, which would provide help with transportation costs. I was turned down. My son isn't 16 years old yet.

There is no allocation of resources for kids with special needs who live with their biological parents, from either the Ministry of Social Services or the Ministry for Children and Families. If a special needs child is in foster care, they receive up to $1500 a month. But if the child is cared for at home, there is only $900 for the family unit.

I began having problems with my body seizing up. I was on painkillers, anti-inflammatories and anti-depressants. I kept turning to the Ministry for help but they kept sending me out the door and calling the police. The louder I got due to frustration and grief, the worse I was treated. Finally, the Ministry phoned the police and I was arrested.

The three days following my arrest, I made four visits to Emergency. On two of those visits, I was denied medical attention; the doctor on call assumed without testing that I was a drug addict. On the fourth trip, I was denied medical attention until the police were called when I refused to leave. The attention that I got was a two-week committal to the psychiatric unit. During that stay, it finally became apparent to the Ministry and the other powers-that-be that my need for help was real. I had been reacting sanely to an insane situation.

Long-term barriers to financial independence

I cannot commit to full-time employment

- sole management of my son's health plan e.g.: specialist appointments, therapy appointments, extracurricular activities and pursuit of funding.
- my physical health: most are leftovers from multiple motor vehicle accidents.
- my emotional wellbeing: stress, grief, recurring periods of depression.

Government policy barriers:

- no earnings exemption for part-time employment.
- ineligibility for Fuel Tax Number.
- ineligibility for Child Disability Tax Credit.

Lack of child support:

- due to Legal Aid cuts, I had no representation to retain 50% custody of the two older kids.
- once custody was reduced to 45%, maintenance enforcement dropped their application for child support.
- the father of my special needs child is exempt from seeking employment, in spite of having the child only eight days a month; the Ministry of Social Services is allowing this to happen.

Lack of education and training:
- at most I can only work part-time; therefore, repayment of a student loan is not feasible.

I never got on my feet after one event until I was faced with another. Through all those years I was always afraid I wouldn't be able to feed the kids or I would have to move again; or I would feel ashamed and guilty when I couldn't buy them back-to-school clothes. Now I fear that without adequate financial support, I will be unable to meet the needs of my disabled child. On top of that, I need to be in top physical and mental shape in order to meet my son's future needs. There are no resources available to help support my health.

Poverty is a form of abuse. Not only do I want the system changed regarding poverty, but I must see it change with regard to sufficient support for families with a special needs child. Setting human costs of grief, fear and lack of support aside, raising a child with DMD is very expensive. As my son's health deteriorates, he will need help with all personal care and mobility.

The most cost-efficient way is to keep me, Mom, healthy enough to provide most of his care.

Since my hospital release, I have experienced support and encouragement from many different sources: inclusion in the church community, a positive social environment, new friendships, and practical help. As well, my extended family has a new appreciation for the challenges that I face and are very supportive. The family pooled their resources and bought a wheelchair-accessible house, charging me the rent that I can afford.

The community centre has continued to keep swimming affordable. A sponsor has come forward to support my son's therapeutic riding. A local music school has provided a scholarship for my son to attend.

I now have the support of a poverty advocate. I have completed Horizons' Employment Program and have secured positive part-time employment. I am hoping that once my son starts Grade 1, I will find other part-time employment and become self-supporting.

Elysia

Method: Interview

I've always said, When I get out of this, I will advocate for struggling women. Because the system stinks. When I read the goals of the project, I thought: I can have my voice heard. I can work with other women who want to see the same changes happen, to give women their strength and their dignity back.

My parents divorced when I was quite young. I was raised in a very strict home with my mother and my sisters, in an environment where I wasn't really allowed to be a child or a human being. Before I was my son's age I was responsible for running the house. There was no social activity: no dating, no phone, no friends, no nothing. There was school and home.

After my mother started hitting me, I needed to leave. My father was willing to have me live with him and his wife. I did and it was a life-changing experience. I got the polar opposite of what I was raised with. They gave me freedom, compassion, understanding, *love* and *respect*. I was so overwhelmed by it that I decided to take the world on at the ripe old age of 15 and left home.

Unfortunately I was very naïve and the world to me was just mine to explore. I worked as a waitress. I finished school at night. I had an apartment with another girl. I found my feet and I started walking, and that's all I did for quite a few years. I was free to live day-to-day and make choices for myself and do what I wanted to do, and enjoy and smile and have friends. Because I was free, I didn't think much about the future until I hit my early 20s. At that point, I fell into a career quite by accident.

I was a chef, hugely successful in a man's world. I competed with very qualified men, mostly Europeans, who had studied and had all their certificates and attitudes. I had nothing, but was just really good at what I did. I had a real eye for what I was doing and a real brain for the management aspect of it. So I excelled very quickly.

I was very successful. And very dedicated. I worked 18 hours a day, 7 days a week. I made phenomenal money – I mean, compared to a man I didn't, but compared to an unskilled labourer who had no formal training, I did really well. I had no obligations other than myself. I saw myself having a prosperous future, marrying the man of my dreams, settling down into a yuppyish lifestyle, having 2.2 kids and living happily ever after.

By the time I was in my late 20s, I had burnt out. I ran away to Saltspring Island to get away from my hectic busy life. I then met the man of my dreams, who ended up being the man of my nightmares. From there, my life went down the toilet.

———

While I was wealthy and able, I took very good care of myself. Part of that came from learning about food and enjoying good healthy things. I don't like Kraft Dinner. I don't like processed food. When you have the time and the money, you eat well, you exercise, you have healthy social relationships. Your overall health is quite good.

Today when I look in the mirror, I can see just enough of who I used to be to keep me going the next day. That more or less sums it up. I don't look like myself. I've aged dramatically. I look tired. I am exhausted all the time — not so much from my day-to-day life, which most people see as exhausting, but from the struggle to provide everyday. It has become a day in, day out job.

It's hard work being very poor. You get the children out the door for school. Hopefully, you've managed to find something healthy to put in their lunchbox. Then you start worrying about dinner. I have two hours everyday when all four children are in school. I run to the bread bank and I collect bottles if I have time and I cash them in. I do whatever I can. Even when we have our big payday (Child Tax Credit or Welfare day), I might end up at seven different stores to buy what's on sale, which takes a huge amount of time and energy. I spend more energy than I ever thought possible, either getting through the day or worrying about tomorrow. Whether it's food, or rent, or hydro, or ...

Since my ex-husband stopped paying any child support it's gone from bad to worse. He never paid a lot, but he always would pay something. He hasn't supported us for six months now, so we have just been living on 'social assistance' and Child Tax Credit.

We eat more bread, pasta and starch than we eat anything else. I've gained a lot of weight, my children have gained a lot of weight and it's not healthy weight.

I have this rash on my arms and across my back that I've had for many years and which gets worse year by year. It's stress-related.

No medication has been successful so far, although we have spent a *fortune* trying.

The last prescription I got from a doctor was for an anti-viral medication. Of all the things that have happened to me being poor, this blew my mind the most. The doctor said: "I don't know if your Pharmacare will cover this and it's very expensive, so let me know if they don't."

I took it to the pharmacy, and asked. Would they cover it? Yes, they would. I went to pick up the prescription and I had this little bottle of 60 pills. $192. That was to last me for one month.

I'll be on this medication for at least six months to see if it helps. That's $1200.

They're willing to spend $200 a month on a drug. I would far sooner see that $200 in my cupboard and my fridge. It would go a lot further. Consequently, if we weren't so poor, I wouldn't be so stressed. If I wasn't so stressed and had better nutrition, I wouldn't have this rash to begin with.

Genetically, I come from a long line of people with bad teeth and it's been a struggle to keep my teeth healthy. A lot of the reason they stayed healthy was because of proper dental care. After the Spring 2002 budget, adults no longer have any dental coverage. The only thing you can have done is have a tooth pulled. Since these cutbacks, my mouth has deteriorated rapidly. In a life where it's hard enough to find a reason to smile, I'm embarrassed to smile.

———

My emotional health is very shaky. For the last 4 years, I've been taking medication for depression. I have a GP. She's OK, but she's not my idea of a dream doctor. She was all that was available.

People look at my life and they assume it must just be so overwhelming because I'm a single parent with four children and one of them has special needs. I'm so used to my life, I rarely sit and think, Oh my God, I'm so overwhelmed by having all these children and no help and no relief and no break. Once in a while, sure, but for the most part, our day-to-day life is wonderful. We're a close family. We have each other. So I've said over and over and over again to doctors, to people in Human Resources, to whoever: *That's not my stress.*

I've always been happy, good natured. I can always see the sun shine. I've lived through hell and come out. I know I'm strong enough to do it. *I'm not depressed.* I'm exhausted and I'm exhausted because

I'm poor, because the thought of waking up and trying to live through another day the way we have been is overwhelming.

It really upsets me that it's easier for them to say: "Oh you're depressed. Here, take this pill."

Same thing with the cost of this medication. If they would spend even a fraction of that sending me to the natural health place, I could detoxify and improve my health with nutrition and herbal supplementation in a heartbeat. I don't believe in taking all this shit that is being pumped into my body, and I've said that to my doctor so many times and it's like: *You're just not hearing me, are you?*

I don't want any of this. I feel like a walking medicine cabinet. Then when we change the antidepressant — I'll say, "I don't think this stuff is working anymore; I'm bottoming out way too often."

"Well, then, it's time to switch to something else."

Couple of months later I'm back: "I don't think that this one's working either. I feel like I'm ready to jump off a bridge and as far as I know about antidepressants, you're not supposed to feel that way when you're on them."

In a project like this, how many women are NOT depressed, but so tired — and I don't mean sick and tired — I mean literally almost exhausted to death and hopeless to death from trying to struggle through one more day? If you're on assistance, your reality is that you live for one day a month.

I have days — and I don't consider myself suicidal — that if I didn't have these children who are counting on me to be their mom and if I didn't have an ex-husband that the thought of him ever getting custody of these children would kill me, I probably would have ended my life long ago. There's a point where you just can't keep doing it. It costs too much to live and it costs too much to your children to live this way.

I tried living in cheap housing for many years. The irony of that is you have to keep moving because your house gets flooded with sewage, or people shoot pellets at the kids, or hypodermic needles come up the drain, or cockroaches crawl over your children when they're sleeping, or mould grows and makes them sick. You have to move a lot because you can only take so much. At the same time, Human Resources is telling you: "You're moving around too much. You're not providing a stable home for your children. If you don't stop this, we're going to take them away."

After I moved here from Victoria, a worker who looked at my shelter cost said: "No, that's not OK." I said to this woman: "My children are happy, I have grownups I can talk to everyday which is healthy for me, my children have friends that are safe for them to have, there are no condoms or needles or any of the things that I need to check for when I open that door and let them go out to play, and you just can't put a price on that."

She forced me to sign a document stating I would apply at a particular social housing and if I did not, my funds would be in jeopardy. As much as you want to stand up and say, "You have no right to tell me where I can and cannot live!", the bottom line is they're holding your cheque in their hand and your kids are hungry. I'm in a very precarious situation. I can't work because there is no special needs daycare funding currently available. Therefore, I have to live under their thumb until the girls are in school.

———

I buy as much as I can, as cheap as I can, as healthy as I can when I get the big bulk of money, but inevitably I kick myself for not having bought more macaroni and cheese instead of carrots. When we run out of money, I go to the food bank. They're very nice and I'm glad that it's there, but there's maybe enough for three days and most of it's not healthy. It's horrible in a way. You get your package and you look in it, and there's pudding and cookies and candy.

The way we eat does not promote our health or our vitality or our ability to perform well in any environment. Now we eat mostly carbohydrates, very little fresh fruit, very little fresh vegetables, very little protein. There was a time not that long ago where we had gotten so to the end of what we had — we had nothing but rice and bread — I said: "We're going to play *Survivor* this week! We're going to see who can last the longest just eating rice. You get a special prize at the end of the week if you can go the longest."

———

Two things stand out in my mind which really hit home, not just about poverty, but about the way people feel living in poverty. One was accidental I think; there were bugs in the food we'd received from the food bank. The other really floored me. I'd asked if they had any children's toothpaste. I received a box and put it in the bathroom. My son opened the box and dumped the contents into his hand. Out fell an almost empty tube of adult toothpaste and a packet of straight-edged blades. The blades cut his hand quite badly. It was a sealed box of *children's* toothpaste.

———

I see a very bright future for us. I have a tremendous amount of skill working with autistic children, because I have one. I have gotten very close to certification. There was a workshop being offered locally that was not only another good learning opportunity for me, but also provided a way to network with people that I can contract my skills out to when the girls go back to school. The price tag on this workshop is $200. I asked the Ministry if they'd help. I have gotten myself certified on my own time, at my own expense — at no cost to them. I am *that close* to being employable in a field that will pay me very well, certainly enough to get out of the system.

They didn't have the money. There was nothing they could or would do. I thought, Oh my god, you just don't want to see me get out of this do you?

I will find ways around this, but that's the first step to getting where I need to be, getting the last of the training that I need to go into a field where I can then work while the children are in school, without incurring daycare costs and things like that. Once I have these things under control, I don't see any problems for the future, a self-sufficient future — where I'm not even working for other people, where I can work for myself.

Fallon

Method: Auto

The struggle to unlearn what I was taught as a child has kept me busy for many years. I was born the oldest of two daughters, to a family of mainly Irish heritage. When I was 8 years old, my parents told me they wanted a son, so I became a tomboy. Mother, an only child, whose parents divorced shortly after her birth, had no experience with siblings so had little knowledge of nurturing. She remains reserved and awkward when dealing with feelings. My parents had poor communication skills, especially with children.

My parents described me as a child who went around with a purple goose egg on my forehead from banging my head on the floor, likely in frustration with my mother. I grew up fluctuating between living in a vacuum and having two tablespoons of guilt served daily.

I learned that I came second to others, to discount my own needs and feelings. My sister was born three and a half years later and was the first person I came second to, but not the last. Mother favoured my sister. I believe my sister learned early to be pleasing and manipulative to get her way.

When I was 12, my parents bought a family business. They both worked and soon after I started my first job.

My school years were not happy and I quit at 16. Told I must be doing something, I started a hairdressing course on the following Monday. It wasn't my first choice.

I began dating at 15 and mother called me nasty names. Mother's lack of people skills became evident while I worked in the family business. Even if I had not been present, I was blamed and berated in front of the staff person who had made the mistake. By 16 I quit.

In my late teens, my parents forcefully encouraged me to marry. The marriage was an empty exercise. He said he married me for my parents' money. He preferred impressing the neighbours than his family. After many years the marriage broke down, we separated, then divorced. Neither of us communicated or understood building relationships. He controlled the family money and I had to ask for grocery money, or to purchase anything at all. He leased the family business even after I said no.

My second marriage was an experience in neglect, sexual, emotional and psychological abuse. We had both been married and had children from the previous marriages, creating additional responsibilities. He had a job logging, but quit to move to the remote community where he grew up. He worked enough to provide only the bare essentials and at times not even that. This left the kids without many things that other kids considered normal.

I found work as often as possible. I had to tolerate people being invited into my home even when I needed sleep. Noise in the tiny place made sleeping impossible. He ridiculed me, he never kept promises, he lied and set the kids against me. He had affairs, partied and spent the family money on useless junk and alcohol, and avoided acting responsibly to the point that my mother called him the fifth child of the family. Because we lived in a remote community, the kids had to attend school in another community after grade 8, meaning they boarded with other families.

I finally left to get help. My relationship with my parents and sister had been strained for several years. Still, I returned to stay in my parents' basement while I got help. During this time, husband number two moved another woman into the family home. His daughter was away at school, he seldom went to see her, and he ignored his son. I settled into the basement and proceeded to sort out what problems I had to deal with. After a few weeks mom asked me how long I was staying. I assured her, no longer than necessary.

I had been raised to believe that people on Welfare were stupid or lazy. I was forced to apply to survive. This provided some food, shelter and medical coverage. I was deeply ashamed to think life had come to this. I was a hard worker and had tried so hard. It was humiliating to be forced to explain my problems to a stranger. Although I was lucky the worker I had was sensitive to my situation, other people have been shamed, intimidated and forced to feel like beggars for needing food and shelter for themselves and their children.

After a year of separation, I was involved in three car accidents and divorce hearings were starting. A new doctor misdiagnosed the problems related to the car accidents, deciding it was all stress. Not until I met an older woman who directed me to her chiropractor, did I get some relief from the increasing pain. This lack of treatment left my arms and hands weak and chronic pain in my back. Between ICBC and a doctor with an ego problem I did not get the treatment I needed, causing permanent damage to muscles. To this day, I continue to have chiropractic treatments and regard doctors with skepticism.

The ICBC and Welfare office staff denied me the treatments that could have assisted me in regaining some of my muscle strength. Some doctors, over the years, have discriminated against people on Welfare and also women. To this day I am very cautious about the medical professionals who help me with medical concerns.

In one short period in 1988, I attended a pain and stress clinic and gained disability status. Turning my life around, these both helped me to survive. A year later, an ad in the local paper offered free participation in a ten-week life skills course, designed by psychologists, psychiatrists and others. It was presented by the Native Friendship Centre and sponsored by Employment Canada. The similarity to what was taught at the pain and stress clinic surprised me. One interesting thing that would not be included in a non-native community program was the inclusion of the spiritual aspect of healing and self-awareness.

I enjoyed this program so much that I asked rehab services (provided by Welfare) to send me to Edmonton to the teaching or Coach level. They actually did this! When I returned, I had the opportunity to work for a short while. Just prior to leaving for Alberta, a car rear-ended me and I put in a claim with ICBC. This took several years to process.

ICBC is well known for the lack of actual help they provide. At the time, I was unfamiliar with the denial of benefits that is now common. They will also deceive clients and defraud the client of needed help. ICBC seems more interested in assisting lawyers to become wealthy than in providing protection for those in need.

After this, in 1991, I became again unemployed. On receiving a settlement (for the fourth accident) from ICBC, I took some courses, including certification in Neuro Linguistics Programming.

When no job or funding could be found to create employment, I requested further education. What I wanted and what they would provide were very different. I was unaware at the time that I could appeal the rehab consultant's decision on the education I should have. Had I known the process, I would have had the opportunity to become employed as a counsellor. Training in counselling would have fit my physical disabilities. However the rehab consultant would not communicate or listen to me in regards to my physical limitations. When I finished the training he provided me, thus becoming a social service worker with a certificate, the main employer was the Ministry of Human Resources. In other areas of employment, there were no jobs available in the region or that I was physically able to handle.

If rehab services had not lied and had provided the education of my choice and a full time tutor, I would have become gainfully employed. I would have been off the system. The staff of MHR deny medical entitlements, telling you they cannot give you what you need, even when they know they can. This was the case with the massage therapy or physio treatments that would have helped.

The rehab officer informed me that he would not support me in another program. It was not until I requested my file from the Ministry of Advanced Education that I became aware that he had been the source of the problem and the lie. Because he was away when the request for the file went through, he could not black out his remarks. Others were given the education that suited their limitations. I have met people who Rehab services have paid to go through law school, BSW's and medical school.

However I have found an alternate source of funding and continued on with my schooling. I returned to school part-time and, at this time, am only a few credits short of a general BA. Then I began doing advocacy, but not in a way the rehab guy had intended. I thought: I have this training and knowledge so I might as well use it. I did with a vengeance.

As a community advocate I became knowledgeable about Welfare legislation, residential tenancy and Human Rights. I have been in the Ministry of Human Resources office many times and been approached by people to assist them. At one point the MHR staff asked me not to walk up to people and help them. I would offer to help while the staff was giving someone a bad time.

Many people believe the Government is benevolent and is there to help the people. However, when someone is forced to become involved with Welfare they soon find out that they are sadly mistaken. The legislation that governs Welfare has not been easy to find. Though still not easy, it is available on the Internet.

I have heard the staff lying to people and offered to help them on the spot, I have been pointed to while in the office on my own business and offered my phone number to call me later. One man, married with three kids — one had epilepsy — called crying: he had an eviction notice, no food and only one dose of medication for his epileptic child. The MHR staff would not help him, nor would they respond to my calls. I wrote a letter to then Premier Mr. Dosanjh that opened with: "I believe it's against the law to starve children in BC".

I have helped many people to get off the system and many others to overcome their fear of the MHR staff.

The Welfare staff often lie, use denial and intimidate people; they try to shame them for wanting food and shelter. They send them in search of documentation that the office has on file. They forget they are there to serve the people. They forget they have a code of ethics. The staff will tell people they do not have medical coverage or that they are not entitled to dental coverage. They are — if the workers have done their job properly. In the last few years, the employees have had to become even more extreme in the denials because the legislation changed. The enforcement of the Welfare laws are punitive and the systemic abuse that has always been a part of the Welfare system seems just short of recreating poor houses like those in England a century ago.

My health was further undermined by the MHR staff lying about health benefits. Social workers are taught how the lack of proper food undermines an individual's health and yet they will knowingly refuse to provide items to clients even when the need is extreme.

I can understand how people become so oppressed by the system that they never recover. People who are disabled are denied the forms the doctor needs to fill out for them to qualify. They stay stuck on the system because they cannot feed themselves well enough to overcome medical problems or do not know how to access employment training. The clients often lose their self esteem, especially if they know the workers have given the same item to other clients. Many get discouraged fighting to have their needs filled or depressed from being a part of some political game, or watching their kids go without. This assures the bureaucracy has jobs and many people end up helpless or hopeless and depressed. Our political systems seem to be based on oppression. I believe that there are a great many people who never develop to their maximum potential but are stunted by assumptions and delusions.

Many people do not associate with those on Welfare or income assistance. The hardest part of this is the judgmental attitude of my family, who blames me for remaining on disability. My sister seems to think she can talk down to me. My mother does not want to hear about my experiences and those I help. My family does not explain their attitude. They believe there are jobs and that people who aren't lazy just go and find one. They don't hear that there are over 200,000 people with no employment. Many people do not understand that changes in the job market make employment impossible without retraining.

Many of those who once stood in judgement have family on Welfare. My neighbour, a disabled women, her family look down their noses because she receives disability allowance and does not work. Many are excluded by the lack of access or knowledge of their rights. Systemic abuse and neglect prevents them from participating in their community. Those who are responsible adults with children do not spend their time or money on clothes or entertainment, with the exception of TV for the kids. With the laws on child abuse, I am surprised that the Welfare rates and benefits are so low. Communities do not want to see what they are doing to the children.

I was hoping to gain enough education to become a counsellor, however I am so tired at this point the thought of trying to finish my BA is overwhelming. Recently I took a spill, putting my back out again and must rebuild the bit of strength it had. If the government changed, maybe funding would be returned for protecting those who are forced to apply for income assistance to prevent starvation.

If I could change the system, it would adhere to Canada's image. I'd create a Guaranteed Livable Income. Those who could be seen to be discriminatory, judgmental or in any way cheating a citizen of the necessities of life would be sent to jail. I would make a "to hell with you as long as I'm alright" attitude illegal. Canada and BC have been reprimanded by the United Nations for Human Rights violations to Women, First Nations and those on Low Income. The government is responsible for but does not protect children or anyone in real need.

Glenna

Method: Interview

The toughest thing about living in poverty is constantly being on the edge. I am never relaxed or complacent, because I must always be thinking ahead. What makes the situation worse is having to deal with the bureaucracy. It is demoralizing and soul destroying.

My dad was a charismatic Christian who walked the talk. During WWII, he enlisted as a conscientious objector, working with the Red Cross on the front lines in Europe. While stationed in England, he met my mother, who was 14. Dad was 26. They married, returned to BC and started a family. I was the middle child of five.

Dad wanted to work in the prison system but was told he was too old, so he worked as a janitor. He was an artist and ran a rock club. Among the things he designed was the tiara for a major beauty pageant. My mom worked as a housecleaner.

I was fortunate with the family I had. The equality was always there. There was no 'the boys do the garbage and the girls do the kitchen'. I was *not* a tomboy. I didn't like being called that. So what if I played in trees and I got my clothes dirty? I was a girl. I was also a cheeky little thing.

I was not my mother's favourite child. I wouldn't conform, I guess. Mostly quiet, when I did speak up I would speak the truth and that would upset people.

I didn't conform at high school either: I wouldn't wear my hair in the backcomb beehives they were wearing, or wear mini skirts. I wouldn't do the nail polish and high heels.

We were also poor. Clothes used to come into the house in plastic bags. We'd get what we needed and pass the bags on to the next neighbour who needed them. My parents made it OK to be poor. While we were the poorest on the block, our lifestyle was livable. Dad grew a garden on half an acre and fed the five kids over the winter. The only thing we bought in winter was meat, and we traded stuff like eggs and cheese.

I'd selected the Academic stream in high school, which set me on track to go to University. In Grade 10, I was having trouble with math and asked the teacher for some help. How she responded

Glenna

changed the direction of my life: "If you can't do this', she said, 'you might as well get out right now'. I had to take a Commercial math course instead. The Commercial stream led to vocational training. It meant earning a living by being a secretary or a nurse or by doing a job versus having a career. Going to University had been an option. I'd wanted that option.

I was quite a loner in school, but not lonely.

I would sit quietly until I couldn't stand what was going on anymore. In Grade 11, for example, one of the English teachers was teaching all this heavy stuff. Everything was negative; all the poems were dark. I asked her: 'What are we doing here? Are we doing English, or are we going to be depressed?'

We had a Grade 12 teacher who used to stand on his desk and tell us how stupid we were: 'You guys are a bunch of lame brain, blah, blah, blah, blah, blah'. I sat there and sat there. Finally one day, I got up and stood on the desk like he did and said: 'You guys are just terrible students! You're going to listen to this guy dump on you?' I turned around and told him what I thought of him. I didn't know anyone in that class, but after I left the room and went to the washroom, every one of the kids trickled out of the class too. In that way, there was some support for what I was doing, but I didn't make friends. I ended up with one girlfriend in high school and I still know her today.

In my 17th year, my Dad became ill with lymphatic cancer. That year, I was to graduate. I'd been getting excellent marks and couldn't see myself writing tests. I went to the Principal, who knew my dad and knew the family. He said, 'We can't make any exceptions'. I went to each teacher. All except my English teacher refused to answer me. That was the end of school. By then I was fed up with it. School was like jail.

Nine months after Dad got cancer, he was dead. The family dispersed.

When I left home and set out into the world at 17, I believed I could do whatever I wanted. I believed that I'd get paid for the work that I did. I believed that I'd be recognized for my abilities. It didn't matter the body I was in and it didn't matter the clothes I was wearing.

By 17, I was going to night school and was a manager of a specialty shop, supervising a staff of ten. I was so proud to get this

Policies of Exclusion, Poverty & Health

job – 'I'm bringing money home now, Mom' – but my mother wanted me out of the house.

One of the requirements at the shop was to wear a mini skirt.

A guy working at the same location used to come around and flash dirty pictures. I reported him and he got fired. He followed me home on the bus one night and forced his way into my apartment.

He raped me.

I got pregnant... I gave the baby up for adoption.

My boyfriend raped me.

I got pregnant... He found a nurse. She came to my apartment and shot soap bubbles into my uterus. I laid there for two days, bleeding. The blood soaked two mattresses. To this day, I can't sleep in a bed.

———

I was about 18 and had been writing to a pen pal – my brother in the Navy had connected us. He came to BC and we sort of hit it off. Because I'd been a 'naughty girl', my mother said: 'Do something right in your life and get married'.

I did. We moved 23 times in eight years.

My husband was super intelligent, but he was also arrogant, a biker and couldn't keep a job. I was supporting us, always with little menial jobs. His dad offered us a house in Ontario, if we paid the small mortgage. We didn't get the house because my husband kept getting fired. He knew more than everybody, would show up in his leathers at work, or wouldn't conform in other ways. Each time he got fired or got laid off or quit – most of the time he quit –, we'd move to where *he* could get work. I would pick up whatever was around to keep us going.

I applied for a job as manager of a candy store. The interviewer said he would never hire me; he'd just wanted to see 'what kind of woman thinks she can manage a candy store'. I was hired at a newspaper. I asked for a raise because I'd taken on more than the job description. I was told there was no money for 'women like you'. My next job was as an accounts payable clerk. Again, I ended up taking on many more roles and found discrimination alive and well in small and petty ways: The men had chairs with arm rests; the women did not.

For my next employer, I was hired to assist the paymaster and his two staff. They all quit and I was left the sole worker. The men upstairs, following company tradition, asked that I serve them coffee at the break. I refused and was fired. I sued the company and won.

They had to apologize, reinstate me and rewrite the coffee making procedures. When the job became available again, they did not offer it to me. I sued again. I won — again. It was the first successful case of that kind in Canada.

My little sister came to live with us. My husband decided to go to University. I was working in a factory to support us all. I found out later that he was not attending University. He was just taking the car to hang out there. Meanwhile, my sister and I were hitchhiking into town so I could go to work and she could go to school. I quit my job and told him, 'It's *your* turn'.

I put myself through two years of college, aced the program — Mental Retardation Counsellor — and got offered jobs all over the place. While attending school, I managed two pizza shops, coordinated a senior citizen's centre, and was night school secretary for the local outreach program. I'd also had a baby.

After graduation, I became Interim Director for an association for the mentally challenged. I had to go with a male Board member to make a presentation to the local city council because women weren't allowed.

My husband went for Air Traffic Control training. Of course, I was supporting him through that too. I became pregnant again. He got fired.

Then we went on Welfare. Since I'd just had my second baby, I couldn't work. He'd take off in the car, supposedly looking for work. I'd bicycle — with the little guy in the back, the baby in a pouch in the front — about four miles to the daycare, because I needed a break. Then I'd come back home, put the youngest one to bed and sit on the end of the bed until it was time to go and pick up the two-year-old.

I wanted out.

Not long after, a minister advised us to separate. I had a three-month-old baby and a two-year-old toddler. I was working again, as a cashier in a grocery store, and I was pursuing my profession.

The landlords would not rent to a woman alone with two children. I had to take my brother-in-law with me house hunting. I lied and told one landlord that my husband had died, that I'd received a large insurance package and that my brother-in-law would help me with the 'manly' chores. I got the house.

Living in Ontario had exhausted me. A volunteer position came up on Vancouver Island. It involved living in a closed community with persons with multiple handicaps. I sold everything, threw what I had

Policies of Exclusion, Poverty & Health

left into a car, rented a six foot trailer and dragged my stuff across the country. It took eight days, with my baby to nurse along the way. It was exhausting.

I stopped in to see my mom. She was glad I wouldn't be living close by. She didn't like my biggest boy. The little one was too little to dislike.

By the time my boys were 3 and 6, I'd moved into a small house in the nearest village and began to recover from mental exhaustion and pelvic cancer. I let my kids be who they were. Didn't squash them or say, 'You have to conform'. Thank God!

I went on Welfare for eleven months. My worker said, 'I can see this isn't going to be long for you'.

I took up a teaching position at the satellite college, which launched me into a career that lasted eight years. At the same time, I operated a small business from my home, sent my children to school, developed a network of supportive friends and bought the little house where I live today. Again, I ran into trouble with the boys trying to get a mortgage. Once approved, I paid off the mortgage in six years.

I ran my small business full-time for awhile. Eventually, competition arrived and I sold it to a friendly couple who retained my services for one year.

I next secured a seasonal part-time position at a local greenhouse, which I've held for eleven years. During that time, my sons prepared to leave home and I became involved with a lovely man. I asked him to move in with me.

Then I began to feel depressed again.

One winter, again exhausted, I took a Basic Construction course. I spent six months with my brother in BC's interior, where we built a house off the grid. It is entirely self-contained. I returned to the Island refreshed and confident that my life's experiences would be used to assist others living on the edge.

———

Being on the edge is saying 'no' a lot:
    No, you can't have that.
    No, you can't go.
    No, you can't buy those shoes; the secondhand pair will have to do.
    No, you can't have a party.
    No, you can't go camping.

It's a lot of planning ahead and knowing exactly where your money's going to go. Then with teenagers, it's how much they eat, the clothes they go through. Toys. No bicycles because no helmets. Extra-curricular things: $20 here; $20 there; you have to have this, you have to have that. All went by the sidelines. Always they were in secondhand clothes. My kids didn't care, because I didn't.

I am tired. I have been working since I was 14. When I retire at 65, I'm going to have this little tiny government handout. It won't matter how resourceful I've been. There's no financial reward for that. I should have been contributing to Canada Pension while I was working at all those part-time jobs, or while I was self-employed. But with two kids to feed, I couldn't afford to think about my future.

I am one of the working poor. The reward for that is more poorness. It's, 'Sorry lady, you did a really good job. You raised those kids. You were only on Welfare for eleven months. Good for you, good for you – here are your pennies'.

I could sell my house, but then I'd be out there. What is the point of that? And where's the reward?

I am now in private practice as a support counsellor for persons living with multiple disabilities, their caregivers and their families. I also have a permanent part-time position to cover the times that I don't have counselling contracts. So again, all these little things.

I live a life of voluntary simplicity, have few clothes, very little furniture, no TV or computer and was car free for ten years. I am involved with three diverse organizations in my community.

I'm proud of what I've done. My sons are good men. They are non-conformists. They speak up too. I'm proud of where I've come from. I had many, many, many self-doubts, especially around raising my kids on my own and standing up to what other people thought I should be doing with them. The fight takes a lot. I'm exhausted. I'm just exhausted.

All my life I've been an artist, right from a tiny little person. That's what I want to do. I encourage other women to do their own thing, to speak their own mind, and to stand up against the boy stuff.

Halona

Method: Interview

My parents are First Nations. My dad is half Italian. I have two brothers. When my parents met in Vancouver, they had each come from a small reservation, but they decided they wanted their children raised in the city. When I was 8, my parents separated. We never saw them fight, we didn't know there were problems, nobody explained to us what was going on. We had come home from a Bible camp, the house was for sale and Dad had moved out.

My childhood was great until then. I was Daddy's little girl and my family was quite well off. For Christmases, I remember this tiny little tree and just a mountain of presents. In pictures of my teen years, I might have two or three presents on my lap.

When I was 13, my dad moved back to the reservation. That's when things really went wrong for me. My mom was always wasted, her boyfriends were hitting on me, my older brother was a pervert, my kid brother... I didn't know what was happening to him. When I was about 14, I witnessed something between them. Years later the family found out the secret that my older brother had been sexually abusing my kid brother.

Supposedly during her pregnancy with me, my mom behaved, but I was supposed to be the last kid. Seven months after I was born, she got pregnant again. She really didn't want the baby, so she drank through the whole thing. My kid brother has FAS. He was neglected. He was unwanted. They're still living together. He wants to be out on his own, but they're dependent on each other and she doesn't want to let him go. He's in the northern part of the Island so I don't really see him. My older brother is living on the Mainland. I have nothing to do with him either. He tried a few things on me. Then he targeted my kid brother. Because I have a little girl, I don't trust either of them around her.

One of my early childhood dreams was to be a veterinarian and help animals. When I was 8 – just before the family broke up – I wanted to be a casino dealer. After I was 8, I just wanted out of my family. I did everything to stay out of the house. I got involved in music as a way to travel, to socialize with other kids and to get out of being at home. I didn't really have any goals anymore. I only wanted to get through school. Graduating was important because no one else in the family had graduated.

I liked learning, but then when I was 15 I got involved with a married man. I started skipping class, ditching my friends. I did pursue charges years later, but Crown Counsel said that I had waited too long. I'm still working through it. He was a father figure, a good friend. He started saying, 'When I was 15 I wish I'd had an adult to educate me sexually'. I was afraid if I said no, he wouldn't be my friend anymore.

Halfway through grad year, I got to move in with my dad. He was everything that my mom wasn't. He went to my parent/teacher interviews, he came to my ball practices, he came to my concerts. He showed interest in everything I did. He said, 'You gotta do your work, you gotta do your work'. There's a part of me that wishes that had happened sooner. Maybe I would have had better grades when I graduated. My mom kept saying, 'You're too smart, I don't need to see your teachers'. But she didn't see me going downhill. I barely passed.

After I graduated, I worked and travelled for a year, then went to college. I married a man who was 26 years older than me. The marriage lasted seven months. When I look back, almost all my relationships have been with men 17 to 27 years older.

Starting when I was about 22, I was with the casino industry for eight years. My father was a gambler. The first time I looked into a casino, on a very early trip down South with my family, I wanted to be a dealer – the flashing lights, the clink, clink, clink... Later, when I was in college and working in a bakery, I saw an ad in the paper for a blackjack dealer training course. I took the course, finished in the top three, ended up getting a job three months later and stayed for a total of four and a half years.

The dealers made it look easy. You worked independently. You got to entertain your customers. You would be dealing with large amounts of money. There was a certain style and grace that went with it. You got to wear a white tuxedo shirt and a bow tie. I found it very flashy. I got to be part of the game, but I was guaranteed a paycheque. I was guaranteed tips. I wouldn't lose my own money.

I could see myself working my way up to management.

I left Vancouver in January '97 to work on the cruise ships. There were so many times I'd come into port and look at this huge ship and think, *This is my home!* It just blew my mind. Everything was luxurious: the food, the facilities, somebody to clean your room. It was so easy to live spoiled. I did that for ten months and then messed up pretty bad. That's when the drinking got really bad.

When I came home, I was on medical leave and had ballooned to 185 lbs. At that point, there were a lot of poker clubs in Vancouver where you could get paid cash everyday for your shift. My daughter's father and I met at one of the poker clubs.

Five weeks after our first date, I got pregnant. I did clean up for the pregnancy. No obvious birth defects. She's developing quite normally, very flexible, fearless and seems to be quite intelligent.

Six weeks after she was born we got back into using drugs because I had stopped nursing. About a year later, her dad was no longer around.

When she was 15 months old, I quit the last casino job. My cousin told me about a treatment centre. I phoned and explained my situation. Within nine days I was in treatment and started to understand where all my anger had come from. I was getting my head out of the fog. Unfortunately, I also experienced childhood flashbacks, which were painful to remember.

At some point, I stayed with a friend from the treatment centre. Her place was a party shack. I started to realize: 'I hate being hung over. I don't like feeling anxious when the dope is almost gone'. She wanted to carry on partying. I was getting away from it.

A fellow who was in recovery and who had lived with us for ten years as my stepfather, offered me accommodation at his place for six weeks.

I had an appointment one morning to go to Social Assistance, because I wanted to get my own place and get off the reservation. I had gotten up early. I put my daughter on the couch to watch TV and went to have a shower. This old stepfather barged into my bedroom, leaned up against me and asked me to make love to him. I just about puked and freaked out. I told the lady at Social Assistance. She said, 'Don't even go back there. We'll get you in a safe house'.

By that point, I was down to about 105 pounds. I'd been to treatment. I thought I was turning it around, but I didn't do what I needed to do. I didn't go to meetings. I didn't get a sponsor. I figured I could do it on my own.

In early 2002, I met up with the next guy and moved to Courtenay. I was still on Social Assistance and had five weeks clean. I was *slowly* getting there. That's where things started to change for me. The three of us went to a family treatment centre. We were determined to stay clean and it really helped, but partway through the program he relapsed. After his fourth relapse, I said: 'I'm sorry, that's it, you're on your own. I can't do this anymore'.

My Social Assistance worker, after my third and final treatment centre, said, 'Now what are you going to do'? Because I was First Nations and the school funding was available to me, she gave me the push I needed to go back to school.

I am currently halfway through obtaining my diploma. One of the requirements was that I put in 150 volunteer hours. I've volunteered in several places and always received something in return, like food or lunch or something to take home, which helped my finances. The fact that I had a goal, for the first time in I don't know how long, motivated me. I got excited. I did the Volunteer Incentive Program with Social Assistance. That gave me an extra $100/month and, because I had a goal, it freed me up from looking for work. At every place I volunteered, I brought positive energy to it. The people in Courtenay — where I first began volunteering — only saw me clean and sober. They heard about the stories, but they could see me making a difference. I was getting unstuck. I was moving forward.

I learned a lot when I declared bankruptcy, like how to budget. Living on Social Assistance wasn't easy. Now when I look at something in the store I ask myself whether I need it or whether I just want it. I get help to go to school.

For food, I got active in the Fruit Tree Program. Occasionally, we go for a free lunch at the food bank and sometimes I've got food from there. At Christmastime, we get a hamper from the Salvation Army. I keep the flyers and watch for bargains. Also, we get food from the Good Food Box program. The other day, we went out with the Elders and picked blackberries. It was an adventure and a learning time for my daughter.

I got into the low income Native housing and it is good. I have to set boundaries with the other children living here though. Many are hungry. I don't mind sharing some of the treats but I have to watch.

At the Community Centre, I fill out their subsidy form stating what my daughter and I are interested in. I sign up for as much as I want and they approve what they can.

Emotionally, I have help in place and I am not afraid to use it. I just finished an eight-week life skills program. I have worked through certain issues, like accepting a hug, and I teach what I learn to my daughter. I believe I am a lot more stable. I recognize my feelings;

they will pass if you let them. I used to get stuck in negative feelings, but not now.

The future? I'm quite happy to be single, because my last relationship was so draining. I really need to take care of myself. I'm very serious about my studies. I had no idea the ability was there. Now I do, it's given me more determination to work that much harder. I'm also aware of some issues that are still in the way; and with my sexuality in transition, I have some nervousness. I'm scared. I'm excited. I also see my patterns. I get involved with somebody who is co-dependent so I can take care of them. I don't want that anymore.

I'm determined to be a drug and alcohol counsellor working with teens. I see the addiction: in the alcohol, in the drugs, in the gambling, also in the Internet, in sex, in working out/exercising, cleaning, caffeine. It's everywhere. I've been fortunate that I've worked with some young ladies that are struggling. They are new to the programs and don't realize how much they're helping me. When they remind me of just how painful it is, that keeps me clean and sober today. I don't want to go back out.

I have another year of schooling with this particular program and then I'll transfer to UVic. I'll get a Bachelor's degree. It will probably be in Child and Youth Care, but I also want to consider Social Work because there's more opportunities. The doors will continue to open.

I don't want to forget my Elders. They have a lot of wisdom to offer, so I need to reconnect that way. Whether you agree with their stories or not, that oral tradition is great. With the kids, once there's an Elder present, there's a certain calmness. I watch Elders with really tiny, tiny children that don't really speak well, but they understand each other and I see the connection between the very young and the very old and the happiness that comes from that. There's a lot of good energy there; lots of hugs going round. The kids need that. So do I.

I've asked my dad and his wife to come and visit. Since I moved to the Island four years ago, they've never seen how I'm living now. What they remember is when I was at my worst. On my last video assignment, I showed them around. 'Look, I have artwork up! I've upgraded my furniture and everything has a place'. They've promised to come and see me, but it hasn't happened. I fax him a letter once in awhile and say, 'I realize that I've never told you how proud I am of you'. It just makes his day. Of course, what I'm wanting is to hear that back from him.

I'd like to reconnect with my child's father and also with his Korean parents.

Last night, I did this Gratitude List. As old as my car is, I'm grateful that I have a vehicle to get me around. I'm grateful that I'm in a place where I feel safe, that my place isn't a disaster, that I can be responsible today, that I can be accountable, that I can hold my head up high. The worker in Courtenay who gave me that little push, she's on my Gratitude List. I've been to Courtenay a couple of times. I've been meaning to go by her office, or possibly send her a thank-you card to let her know how I'm doing.

I'm really happy with the direction that I'm headed now. Everything I am striving for right now is good role modeling for my daughter, my community and my family. My message to others is that it is possible. Don't give up! Fight back.

India

Method: Interview

When I was in Nanaimo, they wanted to do a similar project, but it was for people recently off drugs and alcohol. After 18 years, I had more to say about the programs than anything... but, they didn't want *me*. I figured this might be a change and that I could get what I want across, especially to the government and to everybody else. Hey come on, we're people too! We're not second-class citizens.

Positive highlights of my life? My daughter for one, even though she was a result of the rape. She's the most precious thing to me, even though there's a downside to that. I haven't seen her since before she was 2. But there hasn't been very much positive....

My mom was from Muncey Reserve, Chippewa of the Thames, London District. My father was French and Irish. My adoptive parents, who I loved very dearly – they taught me a lot – are Northern Tutchone and I speak that language. My foster family were Pennsylvania Dutch.

I was raised with my grandparents before I was taken away at 4, and put into a foster home when I was 5. By the time I was 14, I was raped twice, once by my foster-father and then by two other guys.

In the foster home, there was a lot of mental and physical and psychological abuse. She put my fingers on the propane stove. She used to strip me and tie me up to the clothesline pole and beat me with red willows. That was by the time I was 10. I had to run away when I was 14.

After that, I didn't know about love; how to love my own daughter.

The way women were thought of ..., I *knew* what they were: they were just an object to use. When I was on my own, I used every guy I could get a hold of. I had no place to stay, so I used them. I started getting into the alcohol and drugs then. I'd get beaten up because I wouldn't put out. If it was late at night, I had to get a place to stay. I had to do it. It was awful.

I realize that's when I cut my emotions off. I didn't want to feel anymore. So I stuffed them, all the pain and everything, because I didn't want to get hurt anymore.

I had no trust. I didn't even have a woman as a friend. I used and abused men to get where I wanted. I had a different face for every situation. If I was at Church, I had one kind of face. If I wanted to be in the political arena, I had to put on a different face and *act* like them and *talk* like them. That's how I saw the world. You use other people to get where you want.

My experience seeking help has been terrible. I was in and out of psych wards from 8 years old. In 1986, I saw a psychiatrist in Saskatchewan and she gave me the wrong medication. I ended up with a chemical imbalance. I was like a 4 or 5 year old. Could hardly talk, couldn't even write. I went like that for a week. If it wasn't for a young nurse in there to find out what was going on, I wouldn't have found out and I think I would have been still in there today. Then trust issues with other mental health workers....

I don't have energy. I'm overweight. I've scoliosis of the back, two pinched nerves at the top of my spine, three at the bottom, a cracked tailbone and arthritis in my joints. My emotional health is running ragged. I have new emotions coming out since I went to treatment. Things I stuffed years ago are coming out, things I should have learned, was supposed to've learned when I was younger. One of them is love, passion, and sometimes they're coming out at inappropriate times. It's just going haywire on me.

My social life is the pits. I don't have a social life. When I came back from treatment, I was in the house night and day. It's hard to associate with my drinking friends because they're still drinking.

I have no close friends here. It's a trust issue. I've just started to trust women. It's hard to be around women very much, for one thing. I'm very picky in all my friends. There are some that I'd like to know a bit better, because we have a lot in common. But I take things slowly.

I don't like anybody paying my way, unless I ask them. It takes away my choice. In the last year, I've only gone to the movie once, because of the money. Other than that, there's nothing. And everything takes money.

My family is all in the Yukon or in Ontario and I have no contact with them right now. It hurts. I don't have the money to make phone calls. If I had the money, I'd visit them, especially my nieces. I haven't seen them in three years. My family members haven't the money either, to come see me.

Hobbies? Right now, I'm back into beading again, but not as much as before. I get my beads from Victoria, because it's way too expensive here. I'm supposed to be doing sets, but if I can't get down there to get the beads I need or have the money to do it.... I love making things and giving them away. It breaks my heart because I can't do it.

I've had disastrous relationships. If I couldn't handle a situation, I'd move. Over 18 years I've been running. When I came to the Island, I came to where I am right now. I've got my roots here now and have learned I cannot run, that I have to learn to stand up and fight for what I want, again, and that if I want to be healthy, I've got to stand and fight. This time I am sticking it and I hope now everything's going to be changed. There are a lot of things I've got to do right now. That hurts because I have to look back, which is scary, since I wasn't protected when I was young. I will deal with it. And I will help others.

I'm still searching spiritually. My spiritual faith right now is with the Baha'i but I'm also attending the Anglican Church. A lot of times they conflict. It bothers me. I need my sweats, I need my smudges, I need that close association with cultural roots. Between the one faith and the other, I'm not getting it. I'm being pulled apart. I want to be with First Nations people.

I'm learning in the last two months to accept who I am, to trust and to join my emotions back to my mind again. I can accept myself now. I am learning to trust, but there is still that edge when I get slapped in the face. I got slapped in the face today and it feels like I've taken two steps back, but I've still got other supports that are keeping me going in the right direction.

I have one year of university. I wanted to go to Europe and be an ambassador. That was my goal at one time. I never did what I wanted to do. I never did get into politics.

I've worked all my life. I couldn't be off work for two weeks. I'd be too restless. I wanted to work and work and work. There's a saying, You work to live. With me, I lived to work. It's what kept me alive. I've done field cleaning, worked in tobacco – even though I was allergic to tobacco – and worked in forestry on and off for 20 years: started out as a cook, then became a radio-operator/timekeeper. I also was a dispatcher, because I had to keep in training for my radio operator's licence – I've got that for the rest of my life. I was also an adult care worker; the last job was taking care of my adoptive mother. After she died, I said: 'No more of that'.

I want to work. It gets me out, it gets me moving, it gets me income.

Receiving public financial assistance makes me feel worthless. We are allowed to earn $400 a month. Anything over that, watch out; your DB2 goes.[3] That's why I'm scared to go full-time; I may not be able to get on DB2 again. Most of us that are on DB2, or have been on it, we never know when they decide to cut us off. Right now, we're going once a month, waiting to see if the axe will fall on us. There are already 14 people that I know of since March that have been knocked off.

It's like it's their money. They don't want to give you anything ... and it makes you feel like you're begging. I was always taught to hold your head up high; you're a person. But when you go into the Ministry they make you feel like you're not worth anything. They can walk all over you. They've got a job. They don't need Welfare. But sometimes I wish they'd turn around and be on Welfare, just for two months, to see what it's like on the other side. Their attitude stinks sometimes and you have to put up with it. I've got about 16 years before I can get my old age pension. At the same time, I don't want to be that age.

I live in a one-bedroom apartment on the bottom floor. I had a break-in. They came through the balcony. If the screen door was on the outside and the glass door on the inside, which it's supposed to be.... All they had to do was jiggle it and come in. I have a basic bed that was given to me. I wake up in pain all the time. I have one chair and I use a play station to help me with my arthritis in my hands, but I also have to get out and exercise the rest of my bones. I don't watch much TV and I never did have cable. That's it. And one desk. I basically have nothing.

I have three sources for food. The one is three or four times a year and that's the Salvation Army. The quality is really good there. Or I go to the grocery store, but what I get from the Ministry does not cover what I need. The other source is the food bank. A lot of the things the food bank gets from other people, especially canned stuff, is spoiled.

I've always been a meat eater. Meat is too expensive down here and my diet has completely changed. I have meat maybe once a month. Or whatever protein I can get at the food bank; that's not

---

[3] DB2 refers to Disability Benefits 2, the second of two categories of eligible disability under British Columbia's Employment and Assistance Act, 2002.

Policies of Exclusion, Poverty & Health

very much. Half the time I can't eat the soup, because there are too many beans. I'm allergic to beans. I'm not getting my daily protein, which I crave. I have no energy. In the Yukon I had so much energy!

I've applied for public housing, but there is no BC Housing in Duncan. I went to Kiwanis and was put on a waiting list. I've phoned back and there's still nothing. I've applied for First Nations housing, but there's nothing yet.

I don't have a phone. I can't afford it. I don't have a car. The buses don't run often enough, not even on Sundays. I walk about five miles to church. If there's an event catered for low-income people, there are no buses to get there. And the bus fare is almost two bucks.

Here, the rent is atrocious. Before I got on DB2, I was only getting $510 a month. They tell you you're supposed to live on that. My rent now is $445. My DB2 kicked in. The whole month I'm supposed to live on $321 and eat healthy and pay my bills. I can't do it.

I need a special diet allowance. Can't get that. The only way I can get anything is if I was paying fuel and ran out of fuel. I've asked them; they say you have to get a thing from the doctor. I *have*. They won't accept another doctor's note. I don't have a doctor right now. I need one. My previous doctor would not lower my medication. It numbs my emotions. We had a heated discussion about that. I was going into treatment. I wanted to feel the healing. I couldn't do that if the medication was keeping me at one level. We agreed it was better that I seek another doctor, and she would be on emergency basis until the end of March. She did not refer me to another doctor. There is no new doctor. There's a shortage of doctors.

I'm supposed to get help with my apartment. I haven't seen anything for that. I'm supposed to have somebody twice a week come to get me out of the house, go to meetings, do this, do that. No. It was all written out by the person who helped me at Salvation Army with the DB2. My doctor, the same thing. And the occupational therapist. Nothing came of it.

I had to get dental surgery. The Ministry would not pay for it. I asked for a different worker. She was very rude to an orthopaedic surgeon's receptionist. She can give me a hard time as much as she wants, but don't do it to me through other people. I paid the $85 for the surgery. A lot of it takes money: to go to a physiotherapist, which I know I need. Everything takes money. A lot of times, for therapy or anything like that, BC Benefits won't pay. We're supposed to be getting $1600 a year on crisis grants on DB2, but we can't get it. I'm not dying. You have to be dying before you can get the crisis grant.

In the future I'll feel better. I *need* to have it better. To me, it wouldn't be a job, but a vocation. Horses have been my hobby all my life. If I had the money, I'd have enough acreage for a wildlife sanctuary, therapeutic riding, and camping for underprivileged kids. I want to work with people who have barriers, mental or physical.

I need a job to ensure a good future. That's the only way I can get it, is to have more money, that I can live comfortably right now and put the rest away. My age and physical disabilities are barriers. There should be more resources. Like the traffic control course. There should be other avenues you can take, if one falls through.

Jade
Method: Interview

I was born here in Duncan and was the top child. My brother was three years younger. My childhood was pretty neat. We lived in Maple Bay. My mom was a nurse and Dad was a teacher. But Mom was an alcoholic too. She was an operating room nurse and she really wanted to be a doctor. I had some happy times in my early years but I fought with my mother a lot to keep her from going off drinking.

She and Dad didn't take care of us. When Mom and Dad split up, it was awful. I was only 15 and I still wonder why my relatives, like my mom's sister, didn't pitch in to help us.

My childhood was great growing up, but I had these bouts of crying and pains in my stomach. I didn't know why. I was just so overwhelmingly sad all the time! When I was about 3 or 4 years old, the pains got so bad that they put me in the hospital. I seemed fine there. I was OK if Mom and Dad came to visit me and were getting along, or they came separately. But the moment they came together, they always found something to fight about and so I'd get immediate pains and start throwing up.

They finally figured it out: 'It's you two. You're doing this to her. So quit it'.

They tried a lot harder after that. Then when I was 10, it all seemed to go really bad. Mom was drinking a lot. They were fighting all the time. It was the pits. I decided I was not putting my mother on a pedestal anymore, because she'd been so horrible to my dad. We'd had to leave. We were going to Dad's, and back again to a rented place, then back to Dad's... It was just a mess. All the time, my mom was drinking, they were fighting and she had an affair with the next door neighbour. That just killed my dad. Finally Mom went and lived with the fellow. I was about 15.

It was Dad's turn to have us that year for Christmas, so he took us to Hawaii. I'll never forget being in a changing room in Hawaii putting on a bathing suit. I suddenly got so dizzy. All my lymph nodes and glands under my arms began to swell and I went: 'Something's wrong with Mom'. I just knew it.

Back at the place we were staying, Dad got this call. It was the cops. It was my brother's birthday and she'd killed herself. How

Jade

could she have? My brother's birthday! She'd phoned two days before, asking if she could come back home and Dad had said yes. Things were going to be good. But they turned out really bad. It started a really big depression and I didn't know what to do about it.

———

I got hepatitis A in Grade 12, so I was in the hospital for a couple of months towards the end of my graduating year. I graduated, but almost missed going to the prom. Then I moved in with my grandparents in Nanaimo and went to Malaspina.

I was enjoying that, taking all the courses to become a teacher. From childhood, I thought I was going to be a teacher for sure and that's what I was going for. I had a *great* Grade 7 teacher. He made everything so interesting. I just thought I'd love to do that. At college, I *loved* anthropology. I thought it was great and I had this English teacher who was absolutely, totally a kindred soul.

Halfway through the year at college, at Christmas, I got hepatitis again, so I had to be in the hospital for another six weeks. I caught mononucleosis at that time too. It took a lot to get back on my feet and I quit college. It was really too bad.

After I quit college, I started working at the hospital and at a cabaret on Friday and Saturday nights, which I really enjoyed even though I wasn't of age. That's when I met my future husband and moved in with him. I was just looking for someone to lean on and I picked the wrong guy.

He was a welder and I worked at the hospital as a unit clerk. I loved that job. The unit clerk is in charge of getting the doctors' orders and transcribing them onto various other places for nurses, getting the drugs and getting the x-rays and doing everything for the patient. And being ready when there was one that looked like she was going to the O.R. I liked to have all the papers ready before they even knew a patient was going. It was a big responsibility, a good one. I liked doing the orders. I liked trying to decipher the doctors' writing, I liked answering the phone and knowing all about the patients.

My husband kept saying: 'Why don't you quit your job? I earn $100 a day. You don't need your pittance just to be spent on babysitters'. I'd say, 'Hey I earn $100 a day too and if I want to spend $20 on a babysitter, I'm bloody well going to! You're not helping me with that and they're your kids too'. I loved that part. My own money.

Policies of Exclusion, Poverty & Health

We lived in North Vancouver for a while. My health was not good, because I had an infected left tube. I had been complaining to doctors about it because I'd had an IUD earlier. This was an infection left over from that, so I finally found a doctor who understood and took it out. I was fine after that. Then we moved back to the Island, I went back to work at the hospital and started having babies.

I was doing fine all those years, really quite fine. I was healthy and it was great until at least 35. Well, sometime before then I'd hurt my back slipping, but I left it for years until it got so bad I had to complain. Before that, I had a gall bladder removed. It was the two back operations when the kids were still small, though, that just killed me.

My husband stood it for three kids and 17 years. He was fed up with me being depressed and having a bad back. He felt that Mom was always around us, that I dwelt too much on her. It took me 25 years to stop grieving over her, so I can see where he felt that. I just couldn't control it.

My liver was acting up because I was drinking a fair amount with my husband — or without him. He'd be out with his girlfriend drinking on his own.

Because I had the hepatitis, I've got the end-of-the-days liver. It's either going to get better or get worse. Whatever. And my pancreas acts up. You just live with [the pain]. I've had codeine and been on Xanax now for years. I don't bother taking it. I live with the pain. It's easier.

In 1990, something like that, after my husband and I broke up, I just cracked. It put me in a manic-depressive state, but mostly depressive. It took a long time for that to get better, but now it is and I maintain on antidepressants. Then I have other pills for my liver and my heart — there's something wrong with my heart too. On a scale of 1 to 10, my health would be about a 7 or 8 ten years ago. Now it is about a 6. I have to take hordes of pills, 19 everyday.

Since December, I've had a roommate off and on. The first two or three were disasters. I have lived alone, but it was going to be so much easier if I had someone to kick in another $300/month. We could live here, eat a bit better and have a bit of extra money. I get along well with my roommate. A lot of his friends come in and I get to meet them.

I really need that. Generally, I'm a loner. I don't have that many friends. I never have, so it's kind of nice meeting these new people,

Jade

but they're younger and I don't have things to talk about with them. Forming new friendships is difficult because you don't have money to go anywhere really or do anything.

My connections with my family are not so hot. Mom was the social person of the family and Dad's just like an old staid English guy who doesn't show much emotion. I'm sure it was a terrible problem for her, very difficult getting any approval out of him, a smile. I haven't seen him all summer. I phone him once a week. My brother lives in Ladysmith. I've seen him once this year. I don't know where he lives.

My relationship with my children is good, but I don't talk to them or see them often at all. I think my oldest daughter kind of resents me. I was cracking up when she was in her teenage years and I wasn't a good mother. My middle daughter gets along really well with me and doesn't seem to hold any grudge. She generally phones once a month. My son lives and works in town but I hardly ever see him. He's just working and sleeping.

I have a cat, which is a wonderful relationship. I guess they feel some compassion, the disability people. They actually add on a little extra for cat food, a pet allowance. But it's not much for dogs. It basically only feeds cats. My darling cat and I live independent lives, but we come together whenever we want to. She'll sleep around my head at night. She's so cute. Wake up and there's this nice warm head. And fur. She's just a great cat.

I'm living below the poverty line because when we broke up, I fell apart. Then so much was wrong with me that I can't sit and I can't hold a job and keep it together to be responsible. So I have to live on disability, which is something like $1100/month. To do that and still pay your BC Tel and your Shaw Cable and be able to eat for the month without worrying about all the cheap cuts... Because I can't walk or ride a bike, I generally walk downhill to ___ but I can't walk back uphill with the groceries. I just won't make it. My back will give out and my breathing will go. So that costs money for a taxi.

There's so many things that you'd like to do, that all cost money or they're too far away or... It's really hard. Like they have something, say, at the Village or the Silver Bridge, a lecture or something like that. That costs money to get in. Or Ducks Unlimited. I can't afford that. I just can't even afford that. If they have something going on at the Community Centre, I can get over there, but it depends again... How much does it cost? If it's more than $5, I can't afford it. I just can't.

I can't afford to have my computer on. I'd like to be online, learn more about computers. It would be good for me. Maybe I could find some kind of a job where I could use the computer at home and do the work in my own time, so that nothing starts to hurt.

Food is tough to make last all month. I hit the food bank or the Salvation Army. My diet hasn't been great. I've been buying the wrong things. I don't know; it's just not been good. With the bills, there's never enough. Then to go for a full month with food, especially if you're wanting some meat. Ahh, I'd love it. Turkey, ham, a roast beef and Yorkshire pudding would be *absolutely delicious*!

I just haven't been getting out lately. My back's been really bad this year. I need to get out more. I sold my car. I just couldn't keep up with the insurance. Having a car would get me out. Or a little scooter. That would be fun. Hoofing it all around town is just not good enough. I generally walk down to wherever I have to go, but I can't make it back up the hill. I lose my breathing, my back goes out and I'm just screwed by the time I get to the top. I usually just go around town when I've got money enough to get a taxi to get back up the hill.

I only get clothes from the second hand. I can usually find stuff there that's quite nice. I don't have a bra right now though. I'd like one, just one. Actually I'd like two. That would be a splurge. But I've got to get my carpets cleaned. I need to get more vacuum bags. I've got things to get that are priorities that go way past whatever I want to do. I'd like to get my hair cut and tinted, but…

How do I feel about being on Disability Benefits? I'm really glad they gave it to me. I was totally amazed. I didn't realize that they pay for your living when you can't work, which is really something. But any monies that happen to be available should be made so that people can at least live for a month without worrying. I can't believe the number of women I've met in the last six months that don't have homes and are staying from place to place.

———

I foresee my future as just more of the same and maybe getting my back better so I could be a volunteer. I just want to get out there and do something. Earning my own money? I just can't see it happening. When I first started the job at the hospital, I didn't need special training, but I do to go back now — and I can't go back, because I can't sit that long without my back stiffening up and spasming out.

Swimming would help that a lot. It would help really a lot, to get those muscles going and tightening around the back. I can't afford it

Jade

now. I'd like to put myself on a program and be swimming 5 days a week, at least. I'd do that. To strengthen the muscles in my back? Sure I would!

Assuming there was money to pay for a program like that, I would do it. If my back got stronger, then I'd learn what they wanted at the hospital for my old job. I'd make sure that I got that training, some computer skills and would put in for relief up there. I'm pretty sure that would work into a full-time thing eventually. That's what I would do. If I could, I would.

Kaelyn

Method: Interview

I have come from a place where I know what it is to be loved, so even though I think my parents failed me in some ways, I don't think it was their intention to fail me in those ways. My mother definitely, she's really proud of who I am. But then she doesn't know a lot of stuff.

I was adopted as a baby. My brother was as well. We're not related and we're 18 months apart. My parents are from Germany. They were very loving, well-meaning people, but I've always thought my voice was silenced in my family. There was 'Children should be seen and not heard', which wasn't as apparent with my older brother. If someone should bend, it should be me. If anyone should compromise, it should be me. So when it came time to wanting to effect change in my life or complain about anything or voice that I didn't like how I was being spoken to or how I was being treated… When it came time to do any of that, that wasn't heard. I felt it had something to do with my femaleness.

I went to the Children's Aid for one school year when I was an early teenager. I ran away from home when I was 16 too. I guess I was coming to terms with childhood sexual abuse that happened from a babysitter when I was 3.

I moved when I was 18 or 19 and went through an attempted rape when I was 18.

As a young adult, I thought a lot of the misogyny and chauvinism and things that I encounter, existed to a lesser degree in the world than they actually do. I was very optimistic, very idealistic and I guess I still am. I thought that I'd end up working with people with my art somehow, that I'd have a job that incorporated both my compassionate skills and my artistic skills. I thought that eventually, like around 35, I'd be happily married with kids – not living a hand-to-mouth existence or an incredibly wealthy existence. Just comfortable.

Kaelyn

To be heard, to be taken seriously has been a major struggle throughout my life. People underestimate me. I go through incredible things. Sure, maybe I fall apart and ball my eyes out, but that doesn't stop me. People see tears as a sign of weakness so *much*. *Please* just let me cry. It saved my life to be able to cry. It saved my life. I think it's a sane reaction to an insane world, a normal response. And not just crying

I'm living in a situation now where I don't have enough personal space. My roommate is my ex-boyfriend. We went through morphine addiction together. We are both on methadone, so we're stabilizing the addiction issues. He's pretty scared. I'm scared too. But I want to be single. He's having a hard time dealing with that. I'm just trying to do it with the least amount of heartbreak as possible.

It bothers him *so much* if he sees me crying. He immediately gets angry.

I need to feel and show those emotions and heal. Right now I don't have personal space to do it. It's just a mess. I need to get out of there! It's a matter of getting the money, a damage deposit and rent.

People *have* given me clothes and I really appreciate that. The Lion's thrift store, the lady there, she'll just give you the clothes you need. I'm very grateful for that. For example, I was told that I'd be on call for waitressing, so I needed a white top and black skirt. She gave me a couple of sets. Not just one, a couple.

I walk. Everywhere. My bike's in the pawn shop. Our car is dead. We can't get it fixed because we don't have any money. It's fuel injection, so the backyard mechanics who are willing to look at it can't diagnose it. I don't have money for buses.

My nutrition hasn't been the greatest for quite a while. Especially when I was living with drug addiction, I was very focused on getting substance. Now I'm starting to come out of that. I'm still eating at the food bank, but I'm being more focused on my health. That's what it is. I wasn't as focused then. Now when I see a salad at the soup kitchen, I grab it, because I want to do what's good for me.

My diet has changed recently in the sense that, during the summer there are salads available at the soup kitchen. That's why I've been able to access veggies a little bit now. When I moved here in April, I moved from the Kootenays. There are more resources and more places to get food, more access to meat and milk and stuff like that. I also had a bigger network, a bigger friend base. We had potlucks and stuff. In a way, when I think about it, I am isolated here. I don't really have that friend base set up.

I have hepatitis C, so I'm supposed to be eating less fat, less refined foods and more fresh stuff. I get $40 a month extra for food. It's called a Protein Supplement. I told Welfare I have hep C and this is what they gave me. I'm not sure if the fact that it's called a Protein Supplement means, if you have hep C you're supposed to be having more protein. I just know when I said, 'Listen I need more food, better nutrition because I have hep C', they gave me the thing called the Protein Supplement.

My major feeling about my home is just that, with moods going up and down and arguments going up and down, it's sometimes a pig sty. It's up to me to clean it and I never know if I'm going to be coming home to a mess. I don't know what the public housing is like here, but in Nelson you had to be a single mom, or a mental health client, or... None of their housing projects seemed to be just for a single woman on Welfare. If I don't have kids, I don't qualify. Or if I'm not ___, I don't qualify. I don't qualify.

We do have a phone. It could be cut off at any moment. I can't have a private conversation on the phone either. The computer's in the pawn shop.

———

I've moved into Transition House, although the first night I went into a different place because Transition House was full. I started a second part-time job the next morning. Emotionally exhausted, I slept in a bit and arrived five minutes late my first day. I worked for three days. For two nights, I was back living with my ex, because Transition House was still full.

I wasn't able to keep that job. I made mistakes at work, I guess. Trying to keep a second job and hold it together ... It ultimately failed. I guess I wasn't functioning on the level that they required me to function.

That's where I'm at. I guess I'm not going to let it stop me. I wanted to have independence from Welfare. Whether I really wanted THAT job remains to be seen. I spoke with my employer, gave them a bit of information about what I was going through. The manager was willing to give me a break, but the owner just basically said No.

Now I'm in the Transition House. I have a few weeks to be here. I'll be healing, resting, job searching, and looking for a place to stay. Welfare will have to help me with the damage deposit and whatever. I haven't made enough money to really make a difference. They'll just have to help.

Kaelyn

I have a good Welfare worker. There have been times when I first got here that I needed things and policies have made it impossible for her to help. For example, I got through my first day of work at a place because I borrowed some things. The day before, Welfare changed the policy where, if you've made it through your first day of work by borrowing things — or however you've made it through your first day — they see that you have what it takes for that job. So if you've started work, you can't get money for shoes for that job.

My worker sent me to JobWave.[4] JobWave ended up coming through, so we didn't have to go through the appeal process. But that policy needs to be changed. It's just stupid.

My rent was pretty much all of my cheque. It left me $45. There are $20 crisis grants for food, but you're only allowed six in a six-month period. I went through those, but I even had trouble getting those. There had to be some 'unforeseen crisis' that I could not have budgeted for. The fact that I had only $45 left for food for the whole month was not good enough. Since I've used them now, if I were to ask for another crisis grant of any nature, my entire cheque would be administered for me. My rent would be paid directly to the landlord and I would get an allowance once a week. They're basically saying, if I need another crisis grant there must be something wrong with me. It makes me feel like a child, like I need someone to hold my hand! They're saying that I'm spending my money frivolously, unwisely!!

They first don't give enough money to live, but then ask, How are you able to make it? The Welfare policies are just as controlling as anything else.

If things stay as they are, I'm probably going to end up with diabetes. I've been told to watch the refined foods and stuff, that I'm prone to diabetes. So I imagine if I stay living on Welfare at $510/month and my rent is $400 and I don't get a second part-time job or a full-time job... Or if I continue to work at ___, which gives me $200/month, and they take $200/month off my cheque and I still get $510/month...

I've been walking to my employer's. It might be easier for me to take the bus, but I'm walking. I save money on bus cost, but I need higher nutrition. And bandages! I've got blisters. I'm on my feet a lot.

Welfare is not allowing for any kind of transportation cost. They're not allowing for the fact that working can cost money,

---

[4] An employment program funded by the Province of British Columbia.

Policies of Exclusion, Poverty & Health

bringing a lunch can cost money, having packaged drinks costs money.

It's really hard. It's hard to approach people for groceries or services or goods and have to be dishonest. That's really hard; and you do have to be. With The Salvation Army, with every food bank that there is, you have to be dishonest. They don't give you high protein food unless you have children. You have to say you have kids to get milk! That says they don't care about my nourishment.

I've made acquaintances through JobWave and such, but I don't have many friends. People that are in my situation are pretty well focused on getting their basic needs met, in most ways. Through this project, I've met a couple of people. I'm also just coming out of a situation where I was quite controlled, so I expect that my friend base is going to change very quickly.

My cat is the apple of my eye. I've had him for five years now. He actually flew with me from Ontario. He's lived in a school bus on the side of a mountain with me. He's lived everywhere. He's just my companion and he's wonderful and he's spoiled rotten. I adore him. He's mostly an outdoor cat, so wherever I live he's usually only home for a few hours a night. I don't have any human really attached to me anymore, so he is my significant other at the moment - as in, 'family'. I'm going to run into problems for him when I go and rent a place.

I did get him out of the housing situation I was in. It took me a few times to go back and get him, because I'd have to be there in the evening hours, and that's when my ex-boyfriend was going to be home. So that was kind of tricky. I brought him to the shelter with me. He spent the night out in an enclosed space. In the morning, Cat Rescue came and got him. Now he's safe and sound in a foster home for kitties.

The woman I'm at the house with was saying, Do you have a doctor? I haven't. It's really hard to find a doctor who's accepting patients in the Cowichan Valley. Really hard. They're saying that I might qualify as someone with a disability right now.

I'm just exhausted and it has cost me jobs. It's not that I don't want to work, but I'm concerned about my health. Like, how tired can I possibly be?! Sometimes I can't string a sentence together. I can feel my words getting lazy. My energy has been up and down. I'm just tired and I want my health back.

I'm going to get a doctor.

Kaelyn

Yesterday, I felt faint and I felt like I was going to pass out.

For the future, I'd like to see help for young women, to stop them from getting into the sex trade: more programs, more ideas about the employability of young women, more things to help them and other women feel important, to know they have a voice. Things like this make a big difference. A lot of the time, whether women are drug addicted or not, sex trade workers or not, we have this feeling that our voice doesn't count. We have been sent the message that we don't count, that what we think doesn't count, that we don't really matter.

For myself I just want a job to go to, a home to come home to, food in the cupboard, maybe some basic things. If I'm going to have a TV, I'd like to have the A&E Channel, because that's my favourite. Having a job is important to me because I like to do something meaningful everyday. I need to be busy. I *like* to work.

Down the road, I'd like my own little plot of land, a house, an orchard, probably a couple of fruit trees, kitty cats and a bike trail. I want a chance to heal from what has happened to me in the past two years. I know I can do that work myself, but I need a safe peaceful place to be in. I'm very proud of my home when I have a home. I make it into a nice place to be. I need to make my home beautiful. I need a home to make beautiful.

Lucy

Method: Interview

From as far back as I can remember, I was told I was adopted, my mother was a horrible person, I was turning out just like my mother, I looked just like my mother, I had horrible hair just like my mother, I was fat just like my mother and I would probably grow up to be a whore just like my mother. Every other little girl hears the Cinderella story and expects a guy on a white horse. I expected to grow up to be a whore.

My dad was an alcoholic. He wasn't usually a mad raging alcoholic, but there were moments. His wife was a mad, raging Jehovah's Witness, which had its own trials and tribulations.

I was treated as the middle child of four. It was my role to make everything better. If there was going to be a problem, it was my role to see it coming and fix it before it happened. It was my job to get in the way. So I was always the buffer, which usually meant that I was the one that was hit first or got hit the most.

I was injured quite horribly when I was 13 or 14 – a logging accident with a chainsaw. Dad was drinking. He was going to do something that was going to be extremely dangerous. I reached over the top of the saw to try and save the situation from happening. He saw it the same time as I did, grabbed the saw, brought it up out of the cut and right into my arms.

His wife tried to deny me a blood transfusion. "She deserves to die anyway," I remember hearing her saying, and my dad saying "No she doesn't and she will get any medical treatment she requires." She had him kicked out of the house, the church, the whole nine yards for that, for saving my life. The bastard!

I pretty much stopped living at home at that time. I usually managed to find myself somebody good-hearted who would take in a teenage girl who would cook and clean. And surprisingly enough, I was a whore like my mother! But, you know, I finished my education, I did graduate from high school. I did make it, not from a whole lot of help from them, but I did make it.

I didn't trade sex for money. I usually traded sex for somewhere to live. The thing is when you're 14, 15 years old, there are a lot of quasi pedophiles – who don't actually want children, but don't want grownups either – that make really good money. I became a wizard

Lucy

at finding them. I always made it really clear that whatever deal I was in, I was going to go to school.

I did a little bit of college and got a couple of certificates for this, that and the other job stuff. No dabbling for personal reasons. I don't really know who I am. I've been trying so hard just to keep my head above water.

My life the last couple of years has been all about preparing for change and then recovering from change. You spend three days bracing yourself to go see somebody in the Ministry because you never know who's going to be in there, or what kind of mood they're going to be in, or how much shouting there's going to be. Then you go see somebody in the Ministry, get your cheque, and then go to the grocery store with everybody else who's also been to the Ministry. Nobody's in a good mood, there's never anything you need on the shelves, because it's all been bought by people who didn't have their cheques held because they don't have a jackass of a worker. Then by the time I get home, I spend another three or four days in bed recovering from the experience.

I'm sarcastic and bitter. A lot of people have no idea that I mean most of what I say. The only thing keeping me from killing myself on a daily basis is if I did, my kids would go to their father.

Mental health professionals are a waste of time. They've educated themselves totally out of the universe. I'd rather chew glass than deal with any one of them.

I had a foster family when I was 15 that didn't want me over Christmas. I was taken to the doctor who was told that I was suicidal and depressed. The doctor put me in the psychiatric ward. I got to see a couple of doctors who said, 'All your problems are because of your evil stepmother. Let's have her in to talk with us'. As always at that point of my life, the adults herded together and covered their own asses and hung the kid out to dry. I was not believed. I was not returned to my foster family. I was returned to the care and keeping of my evil stepmother. That was my first experience with mental health professionals.

Then there were some child psychologists that had to do with our family after my oldest was assaulted by his father, one of whom wrote a letter telling my doctor that the house was messy and I was depressed.

More recently, on a recommendation, I started phoning WAVAW.[5] Have you ever listened to their voicemail? It goes on *sooo sloowly*, like you're speaking to a 2-year-old. These are women in crisis. By the time we figure out what the hell you're saying, we're going to be seniors in crisis! I had one of WAVAW's so—called counsellors say to me one day – I was pregnant with the twins or I'd just had them – "If I knew that I was pregnant with twin boys, I would have aborted them; the world doesn't need that many penises." It doesn't have to *be* a dick, just because it *has* one!

I've got diabetes. I have a very bad back and neck from being slung about. My teeth are shot. A previous doctor told me, 'You're fat; you need to get out and walk'. But what she didn't ask, or didn't care about, was that it was the middle of monsoon season and I didn't own a coat because I was busy purchasing coats for my children so they could go to school. When I said, 'That's just not possible', she didn't ask Why? She said, 'Well, accept you're going to be fat and die'.

The doctor I have now listens to everything you say and all the things that you don't say.

I can't afford to get a decent mattress, so I can't get a good night's sleep. I have sensitive skin and those cheap crappy sheets that we all have hurt me, all night. The budget prevents me from eating properly, so I can't avoid the problems of diabetes just by diet. The budget won't allow me to change my eyeglasses and neither will the Ministry, though the lenses are so scratched I get a headache by three o'clock every afternoon. You can't afford to get a good pair of shoes, so your arches fall. Your arches fall, your legs hurt, your knees hurt...

How do I get around town? Bus, relying on rides from other people, and occasionally hoof. I have been, up until now, getting reimbursed $37/month for my bus pass, but it doesn't look like that's going to happen for August. They don't want to spend the money.

We were without communications for quite some time. Everybody wanted money and I didn't have any. To have a land line with BC Tel (now Telus) is $50/month. I have an abusive ex and I need to have call display. When he left, the phone had been in his name, with me also on the bill but not as the primary. They wouldn't let me take his name off the bill.

---

[5] Women Against Violence Against Women.

Lucy

BC Hydro? I phoned them up and they're like: 'OK, we'll waive this and we'll waive that fee and we'll.... Alright, it's in your name. Don't worry honey'. Boom. Done.

BC Tel, as they were then? A festive monkey jump. It was just insane: 'Well you can't do that. Oh, well, it'll be $75 to change the name on the bill'. So I left it in his name.

Then he stopped paying child support. I finally said to him, "Look, the phone is still in your name. I don't want people looking up your name in the phone book to find me."

"Too bad. You'll have to come up with $75, because I ain't doin' it."

So I said, "I'm not going to do it either and just for fun, I'm not going to pay the bill."

Because we'd had the phone for so long and I had been religious about paying the bill for so many years, they let it go to almost $600 before they phoned him — he'd gotten another phone in his name — and said we're going to cut off both unless it's paid by noon tomorrow. He freaked out.

So I let them cut it off. Then because I hadn't had a phone in *my* name for 12 years, BC Tel wanted all these deposits. Oh sure, I've just got money falling out my ass! So I didn't have a phone and people would say, 'How come you have the Internet and not a phone?' The Internet wasn't a problem!

I used to garden, but I gave it up. I blew my knee because I'm fat and out of shape. We don't do a lot of meat. Why? Money. Same with milk. There's not very much. And I've turned into my evil stepmother: 'Don't you be eating the plastic cheese! Touch it and die, because you need to have sandwiches to take to school'. And now at the schools they've got all these lunch Nazis that watch what the kids eat and report on you. Yeah, just what the world needs, lunch Nazis. So that's been a real joy.

I get an extra $15 a month from the Ministry because I'm diabetic. That's my dietary allowance. Now being as I can't eat white rice, potatoes, pasta, Mr. Noodle, Kraft dinner, or any of the other Welfare kind of foods, I make myself whole grain breads and the $15 mostly goes to milk. That's typical, right? Moms skip themselves and go around in the ratty underwear that you pray you don't have an accident in and the kids all have new socks.

———

I'm a part of Triumph Vocational Services.[6] My number is ____. I need to know that every time I talk to my person there, every time she needs to look at my file, and every time she writes down an appointment. I'm not *allowed* to have a name because of 'privacy regulations'. I *have* to have a number. At what point are we just going to barcode children when they come out?

So you jump through the hoops and you try not to be offended and you try not to feel like just a number. But you *are*. You're a case file, you're 'the client'. You're never 'this person'. Nobody would ever say to their supervisor: 'This person needs help'. I've never heard any of those people in any of those buildings refer to a client as a person. So you cease to be.

You have to have an Employment Plan. Well my employment plan is that I will try to get my problems squared away and get a job. But that's not good enough. Instead, their employment plan is to enrol me with Triumph. I've been with Triumph for five months and they have done the sum total of NOTHING. I get one phone call a month where I have to tell the girl I am number ____. It's always somebody new. The office has always moved. She never knows what's going on. And her biggest question is: "When's good for you next month?"

I'm also supposed to maintain contact with the CAP[7] program. Not a problem; that's like sentencing someone to eat chocolate.

———

I was completely disconnected from the community for quite a while. Now I've started a poverty project, something I came up with one day because of something somebody said.

I'd managed to save up enough to buy a digital camera. With my years at home with agoraphobia, I developed a lot of computer skills [including working with graphics]. I was doing up pictures of my guys and this woman said, "I don't have any pictures of my kids. It would be nice."

"Oh, why don't you have pictures of your kids?" – because, you know, you're completely blind to somebody else's reality!

"Well I can't afford a camera or film or developing or any of that shit."

---

[6] Funded by the Province of British Columbia, Triumph's employment programs are designed for persons with disabilities.
[7] Funded by the Province of British Columbia, the Community Assistance Program is aimed at helping persons on DB2 to become employed.

So I started the poverty project and people that I know can see me and ask for a portrait. I will do them up, including airbrushing if that's what they want.

All these Ministries have their code word du jour, so now they have this *dual diagnosis*. Dual diagnosis is depression + diabetes.

Dual diagnosis is a crock of shit. It's one thing. Poverty. Welfare puts you on such a diet you can't afford fresh fruits or vegetables, you can't afford any high protein. You're stuck eating Welfare Diet: all carbohydrates. That many carbohydrates turn you into a blimp.

Well eventually, as a blimp, you get diabetes and in the process of losing everything that you are, were, could have been, should have been, used to be, could have had, should have had, would have had..., you lose yourself. That's called depression. I would love these 'mental health professionals' to understand. It's a single diagnosis — poverty.

Half the dual diagnosis is depression. Eventually, physical poverty leads to emotional poverty. When you're poor in pocket, you're boring. You can't go out and play. You don't have your kids in every sport going. You don't make friends with all the parents on every committee because you aren't on any. You don't wander around the neighbourhood making friends. There are no opportunities.

Then the poverty diet kicks in and you have Welfare food. The next thing you know you're putting on weight, because you're not outside exercising. It's winter and you don't own a coat, you don't own boots; it's raining and your last umbrella got stolen. You pack on enough of these carbohydrate pounds until you're a diabetic like me. The fat interferes with my production and movement of insulin. If I could just stop being fat, I could stop being diabetic. To stop being fat, I'm going to have to change how I eat and how I live.

All through that I'm also fighting the Ministry — who today, just for fun, held my cheque. I knew it was coming. I'm here, not there, because the line-up's out the door and around the building. It looks like they're doing it to everybody this week.

Manon

Method: Interview to auto

My intent in telling my story is to bring insight and to contribute to change. I am privileged to have this opportunity; I thank everyone involved for their compassion, patience and support. This has been truly an amazing process, blessings to you all.

I was raised in Prince George, B.C. I remember the difference between my home and my best friend's home. Hers was like the colour yellow, warm and welcoming; ours was like the colour grey, cold and uncertain. My parents were the first to divorce within their own families and our neighbourhood. I never heard the term 'single parent' — instead 'split home'. There was segregation that came from being unable to be around kids whose parents feared our family transition.

My culture believes that there are some people that just have to be poor. They were just born that way. This presumption undermines the function of 'all' children having equal opportunity. Children of low-income/single parent/ethnic diversity homes are segregated, even amongst their fellow neighbours. The middle-class belief system is internalized by the 'lower-class', perpetuating the cycles of impoverished consciousness.

A dialogue needs to be created to break down the belief systems that our culture accumulates regarding poverty. Policies acknowledging the devastation and human degradation of poverty will contribute to changing our response to this hidden holocaust. Human dignity is a right to all people.

Any type of charity or 'do-gooder' must understand the role that dignity plays in the ability for people to rise up out of poverty. One method that can be utilized is to deconstruct the 'shame based' programming we induce upon one another. Shame is an old method that breaks down self worth or self-actualization, and internalizes the oppression.

I have been on Welfare for years, born of a desire to be a full-time parent. In doing so I experience one of the greatest tragedies of humanity and in the history of this country. This hidden holocaust of the Welfare system is a cycle of condemnation and stigmatization affecting generations to come.

I have sat in the privilege of judgement. I invested in the myths that people on Welfare are losers, drunks, and lazy or useless parents that abandon their children. I did that right up until I stood with them. There I was frightened, hungry, tired, and incredibly lost.

How can anyone comprehend the pain and weakness that comes with starvation, unless they know the experience? I know. It feels like a knife twisting inside my stomach stabbing at me everywhere, buckling me over in a hunched cramped position. Can you imagine looking into the eyes of your children, telling them you can't give them food? Or holding them at night, as they cry themselves to sleep because the ache in their bodies begs for nutrition? Have you ever heard the grumble of your child's stomach? It gets louder as the stomach gets angrier. When a child is starving you can be sure the parent with them stopped eating a long time ago. Imagine the fear and anguish. It filters into the mind and heart, embedding the darkness of devastation into every cell of the body. Destroying all hope. Feeling frozen from the trauma and the emptiness of not eating.

As the years grow and life offers better, the trauma of past poverty comes back and hijacks any celebration of success. The memory of poverty releases and reminds me of when there was no hope but only the fear and the pain and the feeling that I didn't 'qualify'.

I am transcending this experience now, though I hold it sacred within me. I will offer the authority of my experience to bring light to this hypocrisy, possibly even to deconstruct the myths that enable the system to perpetuate more damage and justify throwing people away.

———

Years ago my marriage ended. I was bankrupt and lost. I reacted by using drugs and alcohol. I discovered one day that I was pregnant — instant lifestyle change. I chose to be a 'single parent mother'. Thus began my journey on Welfare.

I owned my own home, until it burnt down. On Welfare I couldn't afford house insurance. This tiny house was my son's first home and his future. I got an apartment in an area that is populated by Welfare recipients and the working poor. At this time I celebrated my first year of sobriety. The building we lived in celebrated night and day; we witnessed alcohol and substance abuse daily, experienced violence and often harassment from both tenants and the landlord. We were vulnerable and expendable — there is always another renter on Welfare.

Eventually I found a townhouse complex nearby for $100 more. It was safer in different aspects. Yet still the remnants of violence and drug abuse saturated the air and insinuated the potential of danger. At least here I didn't have to listen to the Landlord suggest 'other methods' of paying my rent, or — regularly — be followed down the hall and told how much I 'appealed' to him while my son listened. My son was six years old.

We have picked beer cans and garbage on the way to school. We have found condoms at our school. My son once fell off his bike and landed beside a broken beer bottle. Had he landed on it, it would have been life threatening. Although we no longer encountered drunken souls who insist on spewing abusive obscenities at us, one evening while walking the babysitter home I had a drunken man follow me, threatening me along the way. I hid behind a truck so he wouldn't discover where I lived.

In order to afford the extra money for the townhouse I took it from our food budget, as that is the only flexibility on the Welfare-restricted income. There have been times where we have eaten porridge for three days. Sometimes I stop eating to insure there is food for my son. He notices and fears I will die. One day he came to me and suggested we sell his toys for food. He has seen me sell our furniture. How can a child trust this environment? How frightening this must be for him! How does he trust in a parent that cannot give him food? I have seen the confusion cause him anger and he strikes out at me.

I have gone looking for food. I visited the food bank, Salvation Army, and various churches that offer food vouchers. I had to 'qualify' and show ID. I had to prove I am poor enough to receive this free food, which only staves off starvation and has no nutrient value. Much of this food my son has developed allergies to; he has eaten it too often. This compromises his health and his ability to participate in school. He gets sick as his immunity breaks down. I can only go to the food bank once a month — Salvation Army three times a year. Other times there is nowhere to go but to the dumpster behind the grocery stores. Access to adequate food is a human right; without food there is no hope. The mind narrows, depression wraps itself around the heart, pulling down on any aspirations for possibilities or options.

The last week before Welfare Wednesday, the fridge becomes scant and so triggers my fears. I try to stay positive, yet my mind spins with negativity. Stress increases and I have a hard time waking up. My body feels heavy and I find the simplest things a challenge to do. My son, sensing the tension, withdraws. Paralyzing fear papers the walls of our home. The desire to step out into the world stops. Thoughts of darkness set in.

Being haunted by the tension in the home, my son internalizes that something is wrong with his home. He begins to distrust his environment. Not being able to understand or cope, there is permanent damage at a cellular level. The experience of being hungry on a continual basis impacts his mentality and affects his self-esteem. He strikes out at me. This style of violence in my child's life alters and impairs his development, resonating into his adult life.

There is no desire on Welfare, no dreams. I haven't had new clothes in years. The clothes I do have are donations or gifts. The shoes I wear are one of two pair - both have holes in them. They have for the last two years. Often we have lived without a phone and we haven't had cable since my son was four. Every place we have lived in there has been black mould — my son has asthma and is on a puffer, steroids in the winter months. We walk wherever we go. I state these facts to empower the understanding of my reality. The main fact is none of these things bother me when we have food. When we don't, all these things bother me. They magnify the anger and resentment. The view of life is bleak.

I have seen women leave the system, reaching for criminal activity so they don't have to suffer the humility of being on Welfare. I too stepped into the rank of criminal communities to survive. It is unsafe; the predators in this world don't care about my circumstances. Our safety becomes more compromised due to the escalation of violence that exists in the criminal world. Because of the criminal activity, I could alter our circumstances enough to eat and have heat. I saw women who lost their children to the ministry, from having been involved in the criminal realm. Yet other mothers make it out of bad situations only to have the system deny them support and return their children back to the abuser.

The majority of the population of the poor is single parent mothers. How many are children? This system stigmatizes people into poverty and keeps them chained with the shame of having to access assistance. Welfare is a stagnant pond of propaganda that supports the governmental superficiality to a society that stands on the backs

Policies of Exclusion, Poverty & Health

of women and children, maintaining their comfort zones and remote control mentalities.

There is no compassion or empathy, no respect or dignity. There is no relationship building. There is no teamwork. One person stands on one side of a counter 'qualifying' another person who stands on the other side of the counter — what a setup for animosity! I wonder how many government officials have had to feed their children water in an attempt to help fill the hole of hunger.

The stigma of being a mother on Welfare alienates me from any dignity. If I should encounter the possibility of co-habiting with an intimate partner, I am cut off of Welfare. Yet if I was working I could keep my income. Is not income assistance my income? It is when I am single.

The isolation of being a single parent has got to be comparative to solitary confinement. I can't afford a babysitter. I can't afford the bus to go anywhere and I won't walk at night. If by some chance I meet someone, the neediness that surfaces from being starved for companionship sets me up for being taken advantage of. I have seen other mothers struggling to keep a partner with them, usually at the cost of their family's safety. I have seen many get swept up in empty promises, get ripped off or even pregnant again and abandoned. Women on Welfare are feared. We are deemed 'too much' and feared 'damaged'.

I have heard a Social Worker refer to her client as a 'lying mutt'. I have sat in the office of a worker who digs through my personal history in order to determine my 'status'. Behind her is a poster which states: "I am simply here for the pay cheque." So am I. What's the difference between us? She hates being there as much as I do.

I have a friend who was on Welfare. She got hired to become a 'social worker'. Her character and spirit withered within months. I could detect her beliefs changing, her distance in remembering what the Welfare process is like. Her 'training' washed away the memory of her experience and she used language like, "...protecting the system from 'those' people. It is **our** money they are spending." I listened to her tell me of the people she sees on Welfare. "...women just spread their legs and get pregnant again and again simply to stay on the system." With this new attitude, she compared her new virtues to those of 'people on Welfare'; I asked her how long she had been on the system before she got hired. Her reply: "Seven years." She was laid off a year later.

I worked part-time and Welfare subsidized my childcare. The paperwork took three months. I went through three different babysitters because of insufficient funds. When I did get paid, one of the babysitters called Welfare and told them I didn't pay her enough. I was deemed guilty without being spoken to and put under investigation. My daycare was suspended. I lost the job. No one ever asked me a single question.

The greatest poverty I witness is the ignorance of my culture and the inebriated idea that the poverty I describe doesn't exist or may only be bad in 'big' cities. When I was denied food, so was my child. His safety and comfort became distorted How can a country that has the capabilities, resources, and command of technology that we do, blatantly discriminate and hold women and children hostage through poverty? To me, it's an obvious intent to keep us here. This way the status quo is preserved.

I have taught my child the power of his voice and the might of his choice. He *will* alter this culture by honouring all people, all nations, which are his teachings. And he will honour himself. He is a true gift, a gift of the future as all children are — even the grown up kind.

I just want to raise my son and not be condemned for it. I know I can make a difference and I believe it.

I give thanks to Great Spirit for the gift of my journey.

Aho.

Nancy

Method: Interview

During my life to date, I have always met life head-on. I've always pushed myself to the best of my ability. I have had financial problems up to 1987 with raising kids and living on one income. I was born with foot problems, having to have surgery at 17 to correct the problem.

My first marriage was very difficult; my husband was a musician and away so much that I raised the kids on my own. When the fourth child was only 10 months and the oldest one 7, my first husband walked out on me. So I was alone in Calgary and in November of 1969 my parents brought us back here to Chemainus.

We had to live on $288/month. It was hard to make ends meet. That was for the five of us to live on for a month. I'd get the kids' clothes at the thrift shops; the dairy would give me their day-old milk and the bakery their day-old bread. My kids never went hungry. I got a hamper at Christmas; my sister always made sure we had enough veggies and fruit. I also had a small garden which gave my children fresh vegetables all the time and also gave them the responsibility to help look after the garden.

I remarried in 1972 and life became a little easier. In 1987 my husband was killed in an accident. I still had a 14-year-old at home and I went to work as a cook. I was only getting minimum wage so I still had to be very careful that all spending was of absolute necessity. There was no room for frivolous spending. In 1992 I married my husband and life has been somewhat easier, although we live below the poverty line.

As a young woman I felt the world moved too fast. I wasn't ready for the fast pace. I didn't drive until 1970. I would have liked to go into the military but they wouldn't accept anyone who had had foot surgery. I also dreamed of doing missionary work in Third World countries. But on the whole, I wasn't a person to look far down the road; I figured if I lived month to month I was doing pretty good.

I finished Grade 11, then took a college course in cooking in my 40's. I did a lot of cooking in camps. Since 1988, I was always in charge of food coordinating. I also worked in the library at a school from 1970 to 1988. I enjoyed it until the school system changed and

Nancy

there was no longer any discipline. At that point I decided to leave. There is no respect any more.

I've had pretty good health over the years although now I am fighting arthritis. I have always belonged to a church and emotionally it's important to me, because there is somebody to stand behind me. It is so sad that now they are even taking Christmas out of the schools. In time of need, the church did and has stood behind me. They helped with the children with food in time of need. They helped me get my Driver's Licence, in order that I had transportation. They gave enough money to me as a Christmas gift to get my licence and a friend gave me the car.

I try to eat healthy with a good variety. I try to keep away from fried foods and red meat, as I find red meat, spices and very rich foods hard to digest. Most of my food is purchased from large stores such as discount warehouses and regular grocery stores. I get green fresh foods at local green grocers. I was at my local green grocers' recently and they had a huge box of apples on for only $2.00. They were bruised but still excellent for applesauce and pies.

I keep an eye open for bargains. If I do find an especially good bargain, I will buy extra and give it to someone who really needs it. I also shop at the discount bakeries where excellent prices can be found for any bakery bread or pastries.

My home is very comfortable and is easy to clean and is electric heated but is well insulated so my electric bill is reasonable. To keep expenses down, we enjoy our cuddle blankets when sitting still. In summer we use a window air conditioner.

I attend church. I have a lot of volunteer programs that I enjoy doing, like Meals on Wheels, three different Christian groups, and senior citizen programs in our community.

I have a car but I prefer to walk when possible. I wish there was a bus system in Chemainus. If there was and it was feasible, it would be cheaper than taking a car to Duncan or *anywhere*. The only bus is the Island one and it only comes through Chemainus three times a day. It would also help me if there was a policy where $100 was given for gas to those living on low income.

My family is very close to me and I will help them out whenever possible. I love to have them come for meals and visits. When I need help they are always willing to help; like when I had surgery, they were there to help. They were there to do what needed to be done.

If I hadn't had my sisters' help when I hurt my back, I would have had to have homecare, which should have been available to me. I asked about it through the doctor and I was told that I had family that could and should help. He wouldn't even sign an application for me to get homecare.

I have many community friends and I enjoy being with them. Friends are important to me so that I can call on them in time of need and I can be comfortable with at any time. It's good for my emotional health and wellbeing. Some of my best friends are the girls of a small sewing group that has been together since the mid-1960s. I am the main driver for outings. I enjoy planning functions and helping.

I do not have pets, because we enjoy going away for a few days at a time.

I enjoy playing card and board games with my sisters and family. I enjoy knitting, crochet and embroidery work.

Ten years ago I was in good health. Now I fight with arthritis and back problems. I am not able to do the heavy stuff I used to do. I am on medication for arthritis and cholesterol and both are expensive. If I go to a chiropractor it would cost me $28 each time and they like to see me approximately twice a week for about six weeks. Physiotherapists, which I need to see every once in awhile, cost me $35 a visit.

I try to keep as active as I can. I had rotator cuff surgery two years ago, so lifting over my head is a problem for me now and is a permanent disability.

My emotional health has changed for the better over the years. I am more content. I don't have to raise kids anymore. I have never sought help for emotional problems. When my marriage broke up, I put all my energy into the kids.

Over the years my financial situation has gone up and down. Up 'til ten years ago it was pretty slim at times. I get a very small pension from my late husband. We live very moderately. We don't go out to dinner, to theatre, and if we do go to dinner, it's to a very small, inexpensive restaurant. We don't buy extravagant gifts for one another — or for our kids either.

I have never had to look for work. It has always come to me.

For the future, hopefully I will have an easy retirement and not too many health problems. I would hope to do a bit of travelling.

We own our own home and I wish we had an additional tax break over and above the homeowner's grant. Our taxes are about $900 a year. That means putting $100/month away to make sure there's enough money in the bank. That money is then not available for us for expenses that might occur.

Nancy

As I live on Vancouver Island, a reduction of the ferry rate for my vehicle, even a $10 break, would make a difference when I have to travel the ferry system. I normally wouldn't go to Vancouver for a doctor's appointment. I would go to a doctor on the Island. But if I had to travel to Vancouver for an appointment, a letter from my GP could allow me to travel on the ferry free.

Olivia

Method: Interview to auto

I was born in Duncan and grew up on a farm just outside of it. I can remember back to when I was approximately 2. My mom had a child every two years. After reaching the age of 2, you had to fend for yourself. You quickly learned how to look after yourself. In nice weather, she just put us outside.

We had a 60-acre farm, with lots of space to roam. We used to build forts and we helped with the chores. I figure most children would do better to be raised on farms. All the chores and physical activity would find them in bed early and they wouldn't have time to get into much trouble. I took responsibility for myself early in life. I learned a lot from watching my elders. I used to watch my sister and brothers get into trouble, so I thought why would I do that? The more siblings you have ahead of you, the more you learn.

I didn't like getting into trouble, although when I reached my teen years I was rebellious and caused my parents some concern. Being the sixth child and observing that my parents were not always right in their assumptions, I would challenge them, much to their woes. My dad was never very affectionate. Although you could talk to him, he was always busy thinking about work. He didn't have a good childhood and couldn't relate with you. My mother was very affectionate when you were little, but as you got older, it was up to you to go and get close to her. She was always busy with cleaning, food preparation, and laundry (wringer washer – a luxury.)

I remember mother telling me that, from the time when she was little, her mother wasn't very nice to her. She was the oldest child and her mother would work her to exhaustion. She told me that when she went into hospital for surgery, the doctors wouldn't let her go home with her mother because her mum would have put her back to work. So her grandparents stepped in and took her home; the doctors knew that she'd be all right in their care.

My mother had a very clear philosophy, which is: You don't make children do work. She felt the kids should go and have fun, leaving the work to the adults. She felt that kids should be kids and that they should be happy during that time of their lives. She once said, 'If you lose your childhood you have nothing'. She also believed that if you wanted something done right, then do it yourself.

Olivia

I went to a small, two-room school. It went up to Grade 8 — grades 1 to 4 on one side and 5 to 8 on the other — and the kids all excelled. Again, the younger ones learned from the older ones. But once the children went to other schools, some of them began to spiral downward.

In my fourth year of school, a teacher I didn't know gave us some oral and written tests; and because I was shy with new people I didn't do well and I ended up having to go to a bigger school a long way from home. I hated it and never made any friends there. The teacher who had sent me there came to the school once a week and taught us, and although I hated it there, the one thing he did was to teach me how to pronounce and spell big words.

Many years later when I was having problems with my own son in school, I took him and went and talked with this teacher. At the time the teacher was retired; he told me my son probably had allergies, that he had the same schooling as a family doctor and wouldn't call himself a real doctor, and not to let doctors impress me because they didn't know anything. My son did have allergies and after he received shots for his allergies he settled right down in school.

At age 16, I was in grade 10 and near the end of that school year I got pregnant. I married the baby's father and we were together for three years. It was a terrible time; he was very abusive. He kicked the hell out of me; he pulled my arm out of its socket, and then another time he threw an armchair at me, just missing my son. That was the end for me.

My son and I moved out. We got $98.00 a month in Social Assistance. As always with Social Assistance, that was not nearly enough! We lived in this little place a short time and I did chores to offset some of the rent. Then we moved into a small house and then into apartments in Duncan, which was all quite devastating. I remember how there always seemed to be a bully wherever we went and I worried for my son.

Because I was young, the landlords would persecute me. Within two months, they would raise the rent. This happened often. A funny thing is that many of those landlords later contacted me and asked me to come back at the previous rent. I was inexperienced about renting because my parents had owned the farm and not rented.

When my second son was 5 months old, his father died, so he never knew his dad. It was funny though; my son used to do this little dance, exactly the same as his dad had done. Genetics certainly play a role.

I found out that, like his dad, my son had Tourette's syndrome. I immediately went to the library and read all the material I could find about it. As my son got older, I explained it all to him. It was worse when he was stressed, so I encouraged him to do something about it when he felt the symptoms coming on. I had to also educate the teachers.

My second son was 8 when I got married for the third time. I had worked very hard on trying to make sure I didn't get into another abusive relationship. At this time, I found out how alone my son felt in the world. He wanted to kill my husband for abusing me, because he felt that without me he had no one who would understand him or love him like me. I asked some friends that I knew he truly admired if they would consider being his surrogate parents. They agreed and when I told him, a weight seemed to lift off his little shoulders. I had a son and daughter with this husband and left after five years of marriage.

I worked at various jobs — waitress, store clerk, janitor, secretary — went back to school to get my G.E.D.[8] and to college for women in trades, then into an apprenticeship to do upholstery and then back to school because of my disability. I found most of my pay cheque going to babysitters, and most of the sitters had weird notions about raising children. Whenever I worked, there always seemed to be a problem with my kids.

I have a good relationship with my kids and I think it is because I interacted with them a lot, explaining things and encouraging them to look at things from different points of view. I also emphasized the fact that some adults were not trustworthy and that they shouldn't just trust adults, but make their own decisions about them. I never pushed them to like anyone, not even family.

One incident that stands out is when I was asked by a psychiatrist to attend a group to support my niece. I finally ended up joining that group at his insistence, but against my better judgment. He ended up hitting on me, so I left; but I worried about my niece. He finally got her to move to a bigger center. That destroyed my trust in people in that field.

I went from an abusive husband to an abusive field.

My third son just graduated last night. A teacher told him, because he came from a single parent family, he'd never amount to anything. She had a habit of saying all kinds of nasty things, but

---

[8] General Education Diploma, which represents the completion of secondary or high school.

Olivia

amazingly she's still teaching. I went and spoke with the principle and together we confronted her. After that, my son would look at her and realize she was the loser. Another time, my son broke his arm doing sports in school. The same teacher made him stay at school the rest of the day. When I arrived, I saw immediately that it was broken and took him to the hospital.

I remember questioning everything, seeking answers. I wanted to know why I seemed to draw abusive husbands to me. I read all kinds of books on the subject. I presented my last husband with a list of questions, first on the list was that he never lay a hand on me and also a lot of other relevant questions. Asking questions and going over them made no difference to the outcome. He was still abusive.

At present, I am happy being single. My daughter got pregnant when she was 14. I cried for days; 14 is too young and I would tell other 14-year-old girls that they are not old or responsible enough to have kids. My daughter and my granddaughter live with me.

I have no real social life, but I have shown a few women how to be more self-reliant.

I get the best food values at a local grocery store. Economically, people on the system would benefit if they were given a freezer.

I've never applied for public housing, because I didn't want to raise my kids in that environment. Neighbours and landowners are in your space. They figure they have the right.

I own my home, a mobile, and pay pad rent. I don't think I could cope if I rented. Social Services doesn't even come close to covering the cost of rent, I don't know how people survive. People on the system become liars and thieves, not because they want to, but in order to survive. When you are honest with them and not into taking advantage of your situation, they still treat you like you're being dishonest.

In the summer, my home is too hot. It's like a sardine can. I have electric heat and during winter months it's terribly expensive, and I worry because hydro is supposedly going up. I turn off the breakers in summer because I was told that even if it's not running it's still using electricity.

I have a phone and an old car. I have a computer, because I attended school and got some upgrading. I hope to return to school.

I had a friend once, but I had to take her to the pound because she was jealous of my granddaughter.

If I could afford it, I'd like to attend different kinds of workshops. When I went back to school I was very happy. I like to learn new things. I dislike being afraid of anything and if I find something scares me, I investigate it. I fell into a bee's nest when I was little and was frightened of bees. I conquered this fear in later years by making myself stay in a room with a bee. Bees no longer bother me. I conquer most of my fears in life in a similar fashion.

On a scale of 1 to 10, today I am about a 3 where my health is concerned. It has worsened because of starvation. A lot of times I starve to pay bills and feed the kids. I have arthritis in my back. My current doctor is no good because, instead of dealing with my real problems, he immediately wants to give me pills for depression. He has no respect for me. At times I need painkillers and when I asked him for some he said No. I only take painkillers when I absolutely need to, like to get to sleep after a really bad day.

My old doctor cared about his patients and their health, not about government bureaucracy.

Lately my fillings have been falling out and each time I've had them repaired it cost me around $60.00. I don't have the money and so I get to starve to cover this cost.

My emotional health has changed because of the cutbacks. I find myself trying to make a penny into $20.00, and because the problem doesn't go away, it's a constant dilemma with no immediate solution and therefore it affects my whole wellbeing. I am at least $150 to $200 short every month and yet Social Services thinks you're getting too much. I would love to see the politicians or the social workers live on what I get. The money I get doesn't meet my needs.

My son had knee problems and needed physiotherapy. I asked to be reimbursed for gas money from Social Services and ended up having to go to tribunal. Social Services said not to accumulate gas receipts and that I had to phone ahead of time and let my worker know when my son had an appointment. So I did. Later Social Services changed their minds and told me to accumulate the gas receipts for a month and then bring them in. They never gave me this statement in writing. What I asked for in the first place and was told by the tribunal members that I wasn't allowed to do ended up being what they wanted me to do later. This is psychological abuse. On the system the workers treat you like you're an idiot.

I would like to be out working somewhere, but because of my disability I need to work at specific jobs. Believe me when I say going to work is easier than staying home and raising children.

One thing that bothers me is how the media writes so constantly about abuse, that people become desensitized to it. People will still shed tears when they hear about the abuse of a dog, though, but

Olivia

somehow they believe that people who are abused — whether by a husband or by the Government — asked for it.

My religion and my humour hold me together. I believe nobody is better than anyone else. No one is superior. In fact, I believe it's your downfall to believe you are someone special without all the others. One thing I know for certain is that you can't change anyone; you're only in control of your own thoughts and feelings.

My future? I know what's to come, so it doesn't bother me. I just take each day as it comes. Tomorrow things will be different. Death is the least of my fears. There are worse things, like living on Social Services. Death is a natural process of life. On the other hand, death by Social Services is an unnatural death.

Paige

Method: Interview

I was born in Ottawa and lived on its outskirts for seven years. We were very, very poor. My mom's family and my dad's family were poor as well. Lots of musicians and lots of alcoholism in both families. I had a pretty good childhood the first seven years and have a lot of good memories of my dad.

When I was 7 – my brother was 6 months old –, we left my Dad. He had been an alcoholic for a number of years. We didn't know it at the time, but he had developed schizophrenia. It was traumatic for me to move away from my dad and the rest of my family and was the start of my spiritual loss of innocence. Two years after they separated, my mom couldn't handle him harassing her anymore, so we moved to North Vancouver. She took care of us as best she could. Good worker, always working full-time, but not there emotionally. Basically, I raised my brother and took care of all the housework. My dad followed us and there was a restraining order: I couldn't be with him until I was 18. That was hard, but I understood why.

My mom got involved with another alcoholic who sexually abused me at age 12. That went on for a few years. I had no one to talk to because my mom wasn't available emotionally and my dad of course wasn't around. I did tell a few girlfriends but they didn't know how to help me. I felt confused, like a non-person and I self-medicated with alcohol, smokes, drugs and I allowed men to use my body.

I started running away when I was 14. The last time, I told my mom what her boyfriend had done. She immediately got rid of him, but we never got help for it. She placed me in a group home for six months and I went to an alternate school. After I returned home, I finished high school, which was really good.. But during that time, when I was 15 to 19, I had a steady boyfriend who drank heavily. I drank with him. I didn't really want to be with him, but I didn't know how to break up with him.

When I was 19, I moved in with a family friend. He had been our family friend since I was 10 years old and he was a wonderful man. He wanted to marry my mom, but she said No. I stayed with him for a year. We ate a lot of food – went out four or five nights a week –

Paige

and I got a taste of the good life. We went to operas. We drank a lot, stayed up late watching movies and would sleep in everyday. I went to drafting school for six months but I had such a poor self-image that, although I did well I was very uncomfortable being there. During that year, I gained 60 pounds. I was severely depressed. It slowly got worse toward the end of the year. My life was going nowhere.

I woke up one morning and I couldn't walk. I had pain in my feet, pain in my fingers. Both my thumbs were swollen. The doctor said I had arthritis, but he didn't know what kind. Two weeks after, I woke up with psoriasis starting on my elbows. The doctor knew immediately that I had psoriatic arthritis. I decided that, because of my mental state, I had to make a change. That day I looked in the paper and found a live-in nanny job. I stayed with this family for a year. It was really tough, but I did it.

Still drinking, I met my future husband at a party. There were problems at the house I was staying at, so I moved in with him, but continued working for them. We lived together for a year. I had a miscarriage — didn't know what it was until I read it in a magazine. The one job ended and I started another.

We got married that year. I got a part-time babysitting job and my husband went to school. Then I got a job as a live-out nanny for $800 a month, which was not great but was better than nothing. I worked for them for eight months. At the five-month mark, I discovered I was pregnant, so I stopped drinking, stopped smoking — by the time I was three months pregnant — and ended that job. From then on, I was a stay-at-home mom. 14 years.

We had four kids. We moved a lot. He was always pushing to build and try and make money. We'd either pay something off or buy a new property. We didn't really get ahead — well, a little bit ahead each time but not very much. It was just extremely stressful.

Always in pain. I'm glad I'm not there anymore!

I took my abuser to court, which took three years. He was sentenced to three years but served one. I wanted to stop the cycle of abuse. He's around kids a lot and I was worried that it had happened to other kids. Nobody else has come forward, but I'm sure there are others. I remember incidents happening in the past. He's also got five children of his own from three different marriages.

In the process of going after my abuser, I alienated my husband. Having flashbacks and stuff, I pushed him away and I didn't let him... We never talked. It tore us down and our marriage came to an end 15 years after it started.

When I moved out of the house, I took the kids with me. I found it extremely difficult. Even though he was paying child support, it was hard. The car broke down twice in a period of two months. It was about $1100 altogether and it came out of the food and the bills money.

Because of my 15-year marriage, everything was in my husband's name and I couldn't get credit anywhere, even though I'd paid the bills myself for years. Just because it was in his name, I had no credit. During that time, I used the food banks and did what I could. Finally I ended up going to the small local grocery store and the owner gave me credit whenever I needed it. I was so thankful for that, because I didn't know what I was going to do.

I took a seven-month course for RCA training: five hours of classroom time and up to six hours homework and reading everyday. Frequently, I'd lock myself in the bathroom. The kids would have to fend for themselves unless they needed me badly. My oldest was with her dad, but on the weekends she would come over to be with me, and sometimes my husband would take the boys. Every Friday night, I'd go do karaoke and drink, leaving the girls to babysit the boys. Most of the time I'd make sure the boys were sleeping already.

Two weeks before school ended, I fell down the stairs drunk and broke both my ankles. The other three children went to live with my husband.

I finished my schooling, graduated second in my class and got a job right away. It was a tough job, but I was glad to have it. Sometime later, I went to the Recovery House in Vancouver. But I wasn't focusing on me so much as getting back to the Island to be with my kids. I really missed them. It was a good experience, but I was told not to get in a relationship, to get a sponsor, to work on my steps. I kept thinking, I'll do it when I get back to the Island. If I start doing it here, I have to leave these people anyway and what's the point? I got up to Step 3, but I didn't do my Step 4, a sponsor. I did have a sponsor but I never phoned her. And I got into a relationship with a guy that was in the Recovery House.

I stayed with this guy in Victoria for four months and it was a nightmare. I've never been in such a bad relationship in my life. He was not working his program. I was going down really quickly, being poisoned by the stuff that was coming out of his mouth. I packed a suitcase and went to Transition House.

Paige

Now I share a place with a single father. It is really good. He leaves me alone. He's a good landlord. We've got a big house and I rent two bedrooms. One I use for storage and a place for my kids to sleep and the other is my bedroom. I have my own private bathroom. We share everything else. Not a whole lot of privacy.

Have I ever lived on my own? No. Never. This is sort of living on my own, what I'm doing now because I'm not in a relationship, but it's still not the same thing. I would love to live on my own. All by myself. Then I wouldn't have anybody else around when my kids come to visit. It would be me and the kids. That would be really nice. Privacy. Peace. Contentment.

———

My arthritis has been good for about five or six years. Around 1999, I wasn't coping. Not drinking, but just really suicidal. I couldn't deal with anything: the housework, the kids, nothing. I had a car accident, a minor one, but it threw me. I couldn't stop crying. I went to the doctor, bawling. I gave him my history and he said, It sounds like you've had depression for a long time. He put me on Paxil and I got some help from Cowichan Family Life and other places.

As soon as I went on Paxil, I started to sleep better. Before, it had taken me two or three hours to get to sleep, even when I was teenager, right through having babies and everything. That probably had a lot to do with my physical problems, with not healing – the depression, not being able to cope. My body takes a lot of energy to keep up with the psoriasis and arthritis. I need a lot of protein too, which I didn't know 'til several years ago. I was always on a low-fat kick. Now I'm on low-carb instead and it's so much better for me. My arthritis hasn't come back, so I know I'm doing something right.

———

The past couple of months have been tough. When I go into the social assistance office, I try and have a really good attitude. But I feel degraded. Everyone's depressed. The people that work there and the people that go in there, all seem really down. It gets so frustrating sometimes. They can be very disrespectful. I've come out of there bawling about five times.

Four months ago, I got a red flag on my cheque, which says you've got to come in and straighten something out... She went through all my papers and finally found the information that was already there in my file. Then it got flagged again... They already had that information too. This month, it's flagged again and I don't know why. Each time I have to come in, I have to pay for the bus fare. I'd like to see them have something that shows you how the system works, what you're going to need. It seems like every time I go in for one thing, I get sent off to another place for another thing. Then *they* want me to get something else.

How does Social Assistance meet my needs? It doesn't. I feel unequal in a lot of my friendships because of the finances. They're always offering me meals. I need money for bus fare, stuff for my skin, toiletries and all that. One month I'll buy mainly toiletries and there won't be much left over for food. The next month I'll buy food and let the rest ride. I go without toilet paper or whatever, if I have to.

Basically my landlord's been paying for my food, except for vegetables. I get those from a friend who has a garden. I'm living off tuna and eggs and vegetables. The starchy stuff I get from the food bank I don't eat. It's not good for my arthritis and my skin. I have asked for a protein allowance, but even though the doctor writes up permission to get that, they don't give it now for psoriasis. People with psoriasis need extra protein, especially if they have it this bad.

When they wouldn't give me food at the food bank, that was very upsetting. My husband wasn't going to allow my children to come over because they were eating food bank food. There's not much I can do about that. So they just didn't come over. Also, the food bank wouldn't give me food because the kids aren't with me 40% of the time. They're with me 33-1/3% of the time. Well, how do I feed them for those ten days?

I was going for a crisis grant because I didn't have enough food for the kids. Welfare asked me to sign a Family Maintenance form, because my husband and I are doing our separation privately. I signed it so they could go after him for Spousal Maintenance. I don't really want them to. I didn't want to sign the thing, but I had to. Now they refuse to give me crisis grants. They want me to ask him for money for food. I can't do it. He's hostile about giving me money. He makes $4000/month and I'm on Welfare and he wants child support. I'm perfectly willing to do that when I get a job.

Some of the stuff that could really help my skin isn't covered. I tried to get Dovobet and it's very expensive, but it really works well. It's a mixture of Dovonex and Betamethasone. The pharmacy recommended that I get them separate and mix them together myself. That way, they're covered. My skin would probably clear up with the Dovobet, especially in the summer. They use the sun with it. They have ultraviolet light treatments, but it's very stressful getting there and back, plus it's more transportation money. So, I just don't do it.

The future? Horizons is going to be excellent. I'm excited about it because it's a good long period for me to work on myself and I don't have to worry about anything else. Just for me, to get myself better. I'm very focused on getting off the system and getting back to work. As soon as I feel my mind is ready for it — and physically too, because my mind affects my body.

I love working with words, with writing, with reading. I should probably get out of the caretaking business. I've been doing that all my life. It's time for a change.

Rayna

Method: Interview

I was pretty outgoing as a really young child. If I thought something was crap, I would say so. The first time my mom took out her stuff on me, I sat her down the next day and said, 'You got a little out of control'. Just had this rational discussion! I was 7.

I'd love to be able to do that now. I just got worn down. My first suicide attempt was at 14. Then I had another attempt at 17. There have been numerous incidents since. I've spent lots of time in hospital and been diagnosed with borderline personality disorder, depression and anxiety.

They say, 'What doesn't kill you makes you stronger', but sometimes you feel like you just get more and more drained. I live on a razor's edge still. Right now, just maintaining work and maintaining my health takes everything. It takes everything I've got.

I was born in Ontario, the middle child of three. We moved to Jamaica when I was 3 months old and we lived there for the first five years of my life. My parents were missionaries, my father a minister and my mother a school teacher.

The political climate was unsafe in Jamaica, so we moved to Victoria. That was quite a culture shock and it turned out not to be a good thing. My dad was underemployed and sickly. They chose Victoria because they thought it would be better for his health. But our family was all in Ontario, which meant that my parents had no support.

My dad went into depression and stayed there long after I left home. By the time I was 9, he was really hard to live with. He was always picking on us. I remember getting into a fight with my dad when I was 9 and saying I couldn't wait 'til Monday (when he would return to his part-time job). The stress had been building and affected my mom. That's probably why she started beating me when I was 7.

We moved to different neighbourhoods and I wound up at a really tough school; I got beaten up at school everyday for a couple of years. It was ironic. I got beaten by a gang of girls on the same bridge that Reena Virk died under. Of course, I was supposed to come home with A's and B's. It just wasn't happening. So I'd get beaten up at home as well.

It took me about a year to settle into a normal classroom after they moved us to a private school. But the trouble at home continued. By 9, I had an eating disorder. By 14, I was popping my dad's Valiums.

At one point, they were going to put me in a foster home. I had one year left at school and was failing, because I was stoned all the time and anorexic that year. I begged them not to do it. I went off the pills — they didn't know I was taking them — and did a whole year of work in the last semester. That was stressful, but I did it. When I graduated, I had just turned 17.

I kind of crashed after that.

My friends moved on, to university and stuff. I started teaching aerobics that summer and aerobics became a lifelong passion. I also worked full-time at a fast food place and went back to school. I started drinking and drank alcoholically from the very first drink.

I wanted to get my degree by 21; started off with recreation leadership and moved into social work. I managed to complete three years post-secondary, which took me four or five years to get done. My issues kept getting in the way.

My dad got sick again, for the hundredth millionth time. He had cancer. Working full-time and teaching aerobics, I just couldn't take the pressure at home anymore, so I moved out and lived with a friend's family. It became apparent that I didn't know how to be part of a normal family, so I left and moved back home, back to the chaos I was used to. My grandmother was there. They wouldn't let me sleep on the couch in the house. It was inconvenient. I slept in the garage with the wood and the wood bugs instead. A month or so later, me and my dad had it out. I left for the final time, with only enough money for a hotel room for that night.

There was some involvement with the street after that and I struggled with drug and alcohol abuse. As my addiction progressed, it got harder to keep jobs and places.

After numerous admissions to the psych ward over the next few years, I went into recovery at 23. For three years, things were reasonably OK. I had a good relationship that lasted three years and was working as a psych care worker.

One day my sister showed up on my doorstep, saying that my father was terminal. I cautiously reconnected, saw my father once before he died and we had reconciliation. My family were strong Christians and they used this reconnection to work hard at trying to convert me. I returned home with my spirituality smashed. I lost my sobriety.

I decided to make a big life change and moved to the Cowichan Valley. It was a good move, although I wound up on the psych ward here. I was impressed with the way the people in Emergency treated me, as well as my GPs, my psychologist and the folks on the 4th floor. Eventually I had to get Disability Benefits and got lots of support from my worker at Mental Health. It was my first step in getting well.

———

I've been maintaining casual contact with my mother, but recently that's gone down the tubes. She's still the same person she was. That vicious side comes out. I'm sort of hurting over that. I keep hoping she is going to change. I thought that it was enough that I had changed. That's why it was hard when they came back into my life. I had given up that hope and had carried on with my life.

I have some very dear friends. Also I'm in a 12-step program, which is very supportive.

Now I'm working as a janitor. Work is important to me — just having a place to go everyday and being able to say that I'm at least beginning to pay my way through society. Work is a reason to get up. That's what most of us do. We get up and we have a place to go to work, so it makes me feel proud that I've got employment.

Food is my biggest struggle. I struggle with obesity, partly the result of my earlier eating disorder. An endocrinologist put me on a low-carb, high-protein diet. That's an expensive way to eat. I applied for a nutritional supplement through the Ministry and it was refused. They were paying for me to go see the endocrinologist, but they wouldn't cover for me to follow her suggestions.

When I'm able to work, I eat better. I'm healthiest on that diet. I have more energy, I don't have problems with acid reflux, my weight starts to come down. At one time when I was working, I lost 45 lbs. I gained it all back in a couple of months of being broke and eating at the food bank.

My place is fairly comfortable but it's boiling hot in the summer. I have a negligent landlord. There is no insulation in the ceiling. Only one window opens, which affects temperature and safety. There is some mould in the bedroom. I have to keep the heat on all winter.

With respect to housing, pets are a big thing, especially for those of us who are single with no families. I have two guinea pigs and two cats. One cat I've had for 14 years. I call her my AL-ANON cat, because she's been through everything. One time she was in a kennel for three months while I was in the hospital. I still have her; she's still here.

My pets keep me alive a lot of times when I would just rather not do it anymore. My landlord is not the nicest person, but just the thought of moving — because of my animals and being able to find a place that will take animals —, it's hard. I remember talking to an acquaintance. She had no idea about the cycle of poverty. I bounced a cheque. She went on about honesty. It's not about honesty! It's about robbing Peter to pay Paul. I said something to the effect: 'If the animals are hungry, you're going to feed the animals'. Her response was, 'Well, don't have animals then'. She just didn't get it.

I get around town by hoofing it. And using the occasional bus. I've no licence and no vehicle. I wasn't allowed to get my licence when I was 16. A year later, I'd left home and hit the street. Now it's really hard to get a licence. You've got to have somebody drive around with you for a year. I'm in my 30s. It's not like I can go to Mom and Dad.

In Victoria, the lack of a vehicle worked out OK, but up here buses don't go everywhere or run most hours. That's why it's taken me two years to get full-time work. A lot of the jobs were where I couldn't get to. Even now, I walk home from work at 2am.

I worry for my safety. I'm fortunate that I've got sites that are within a few blocks of my home, but there was an incident not long ago in a parking lot that could have turned bad. Since then, I carry a cell phone, which is an added expense. And I'm feeling it. There are no provisions for employment expenses. I'm making the same amount of money that I did sitting on Disability, but I'm having to put out more money to maintain the work.

I've struggled to keep my regular phone service too. Sometimes your choices are to have groceries, or to feed the animals, or to pay the phone bill. A lot of times, I've gone without a phone, but for me, someone living alone, the phone is my lifeline. That's how I reach my friends. It's also how I access health services if I'm in crisis.

I run out of money all the time for groceries. Because of that, I've got into that payday loan cycle, which is totally screwing me up. The interest they charge is just outrageous. I just spent $100 interest at one place. It started out as a loan of $180. They added $50 for something; they just took it right out. Because of the size of the loan, I couldn't pay it off in one pay period. So they reissued the loan — but then that's another $50. That $180 loan has cost me $280 so far.

I don't really know how I'm going to break the cycle, but when you're working you've got to eat properly. It's really tough. Today I've got to go to work, I'm broke and my next paycheque is not for another week. And now a new policy at work is that they don't drop off the cheques on payday until 5pm. That's another day I've got to stretch this money out. That's what's got me down today. I work really hard at my job and it does help my self-esteem, but I'm getting in the hole faster than when I was on full Disability. It's discouraging.

I make $100/month less than what I'm allowed on Disability and because I'm still on the system, I get a rent subsidy. But if I got to the point where I was earning above the Disability allowance, I'd lose the rent subsidy. That means I'd be living on $200/month less than when I was living on the system.

In other words, there's a financial disincentive to work, but I want to work for the sake of my self-esteem. It's very punishing. It's even more punishing for people who are on regular Welfare, because the Welfare people take dollar for dollar. At least when you're on Disability, you're allowed to earn $400/month.

Living below the poverty line has most affected my self-esteem and emotional health. If I hadn't got at least an increase to Disability Benefits, if I had still been on regular Welfare, I know for a fact that I wouldn't be here. The money factor was HUGE.

It's really hard to get well when you can't eat. I was taking my pills, but I wasn't eating half the time and what I was eating was crap. You can take all the serotonin you want, but if you're body's not being fed... That's what was happening. I was going down and down and was becoming increasingly suicidal. If I had remained on regular Welfare, especially with the pressure to go back to work before you're ready, I would have taken my life. I was on the edge anyhow.

You feel like you deserve to be poor. People who are disabled, mentally or physically, are regulated to a life of poverty. Those who can't work are regulated to live on $800/month for the rest of their lives. If you can manage to work part-time, you're still making $1186/month – minus employment expenses. That's not a huge amount. You're never going to own your own place.

I just don't know if that's quite fair. They should have ways to let people with disabilities make mortgage payments instead of paying rent.

Rayna

I don't like not having a little bit of money in my pocket. I used to feel guilty for that. Everybody else likes to have a little bit of money in their pocket. Shouldn't I? Am I not allowed that? There's all this internal judgement. You say to yourself what somebody not in the cycle is going to say — like that woman who said, 'You shouldn't have pets'. Today's a tough day for that.

Even $5 in my pocket would be nice. I don't think that's too much to ask. I work my butt off at my work, so it's discouraging to still have the same problems, trying to catch up, trying to catch up.

The future? I'd be happy if I could just own a little mobile, something that's mine that I could do whatever I wanted with. I would like a relationship, but I don't always feel very hopeful about that. And I'm still going to go after a degree, but a Bachelor of Arts, with a minor in Women's Studies and a major in Physical Education. I'd like to work with plus-size women in the area of fitness. It would be really nice to be a little more than comfortable and to do something that I have a passion for.

Sheree

Method: Interview

I was an angry, angry, very angry child. What infuriates me the most is the silence. Nobody will come out and say anything.

I imagined my future as a Cinderella story. I washed the walls, I washed the floors, I cooked, I cleaned; and one day my prince would come. He never did. I've had lots of toads, but no princes. I wanted to become a lawyer; I wanted to be able to work and be the Justice. I wanted to be able to say "Hey, you're not allowed to do that to that person!" And have the legal right to be able to help women and children from abused families. I wanted to have a great big home, the opposite of those Christian homes or the Catholic places they sent kids to, the residential schools. I wanted to have a big school where all the kids would be happy.

―――

My father had children from a previous marriage and so did my mother. I remember a lot of the good times: my mother being caring and my brothers and my family all together. And then, all of a sudden she died. That was before I turned 5. After that, my life was a living hell.

I've always hated the way I looked. I was fair-skinned; I had light hair. I wasn't Status. I was considered Caucasian by the Native community and by the government, but the white people would look at me: "You're Native." I was hated and ridiculed by my family and my peers: I was nothing; I was nobody; I would never amount to anything, no matter how I tried, where I tried or who I tried with; I was adopted; I was found in the ditch; I was found in the garbage. That was what they told me.

I was beat up physically everyday. By the time I turned 5, I was made into a sexual object for a half-uncle. Until I was 11 or 12, my grandmother sent me there, for him, knowing full well what he was doing to me. She didn't care: "You're just a bitch, you're just a whore." I didn't know what that was.

Sometimes I'd take a knife and I'd stand there wanting to cut my face up, to slice my body up and say: Now are you going to love me? This is what you want to rape? You're not raping my soul. You can't touch that. I'm not allowing you to go there. This is for the

Sheree

Creator. He gave it to me, a gift, to be able to love people for who they are.

They tried to shut me down. They were trying to destroy who I was inside.

I moved to whoever would take me. When I would get happy somewhere, my dad would come and take me, because my grandmother wanted me in the house. She'd get x amount of dollars for me there. Plus I knitted for her; I made sweaters, I made money, I picked berries, I cooked, I cleaned. I did absolutely everything.

I don't regret being up at 4 or 5 in the morning, at 4 or 5 years old, going to different households and making them their tea in the morning, and their coffee and scrambled eggs. They'd all sit around and take turns talking to me. I'd go there and build their fires, at such a young age. That's just tradition, how we raise our children, to be fully participant and be somebody. There was no 'I', 'me', 'mine'. It's all 'ours', 'us', 'we' in our language. You're somebody; you're special. You're a little person right from the very beginning. You're sacred.

I had only one person in my life at the time who was saying I wasn't sacred. That was grandmother.

I was married when I was 16. I'd had a tubal pregnancy and almost died. The doctors had to do an emergency operation, told me I'd probably never ever have children, because of all the stuff that happened to me as a child. I was so devastated, so hurt, because I'd wanted to have children all my life. My husband and I got a divorce.

Met this guy that I'd known since I was a kid and we got together at 19. It happened just the once and I was pregnant. I was just like, Oh my God... I could *feel* my body change. It was just an incredible feeling. I was praying on my knees for days and days and days: Please God, give me a baby. Just one. To have somebody who loves me and to have somebody for me to love that they wouldn't take away. To have my own family, something that's my own, mine, me, my breath, my life.

I was blessed. I had my son. Then there's my daughter. I was blessed twice.

My son was 3-1/2 when he was diagnosed with muscular dystrophy. I started reading up on everything I could about MD. When I was pregnant, I went out and read books on pregnancy... I think I've lost that somewhere, that get up and go. I'm so, so tired...

just enough to live, to be able to survive, to jockey all the things going on.

I hated the doctors. They did tests after tests after tests. They'd say: Why don't you have a house? Why don't you have a husband? Why don't you have money? Why don't you, why don't you, why don't you? Not: You're doing so well considering you're a single mom and trying your best; your son seems to be such a happy child.

When my children were 2-1/2 and 3-1/2, I was raped. My kids were locked in a dark room and heard their mother screaming for hours and hours and hours. When the cops got there, he was standing behind the door, holding my daughter on his hip with his hand on her neck. My daughter, my baby... Because I didn't say No after a certain amount of time, they didn't classify it as rape... The cops took my statement and put me on a bus with my children. I hadn't even gone to see a doctor.

My son would get a lot more help if I wasn't here, a lot more help from the government. They would have somebody else to clean his room, somebody else to come and do his laundry, somebody else to help him with his cooking needs. Other than me, somebody who's tired. They've told me so. But they expect me to abandon him first.

My son has a medical condition. He's slowly dying of it. So I tried to seek counselling for myself. I'm supposed to be on a regular schedule, but I've seen the psychiatrist once. The Government said that if I needed help and I couldn't deal with my stressful life as a single mother, they would take my children from me and put me somewhere where I could get help. They have tried twice to remove my children from my home because I needed help dealing with stress and all my financial burdens. The stress is simply for lack of funds. They're keeping me in poverty.

The poverty has an extreme affect on how I feel about myself. It shouldn't, but it does. I can't dress like I want to dress. I can't conduct my life like I want to conduct my life. I can't contribute, I'm not a whole person. I'm limited, I'm shackled, I'm handcuffed to poverty with no way out. No matter what I do, or what I say, or who I approach, they look at me and say: You don't have transportation, you don't have a steady babysitter, you don't have a phone. I don't, don't, don't, don't, don't have. But if I don't have a job, I can't get it.

It makes me feel real heavy, real sad. People are so mean and I don't understand.

Sheree

Once I had a two-story house, luxurious hutches and coffee tables, end tables, entertainment systems. I was building a life with somebody. Put $20,000 into a house. All of a sudden, it's gone and I can't get it back. Now my home is a rental apartment. The fridge has holes in it. You can see light when the door's closed.

I'm still ashamed of my place, of where I live, my circumstances.

I have a vehicle that was given to me. But can I afford the upkeep of it? No I can't. Can I afford the gas in it? No I can't. Can I afford the insurance for it? No I can't. Can I live without it? No I can't. So I budget, budget, budget, stay home and do nothing.

I don't buy myself juices. We live on powder or water. I try to make sure my son has milk everyday. As for fresh fruits and fresh vegetables, that's next to nothing. I eat a lot of Native food: fish, deer meat, because it's free. I don't buy a lot of everything. I did go to the Salvation Army. I have never been to the food bank. I guess my pride... I just can't. It's begging to me. I can't beg my family for anything, I can't beg society. I did all kinds of begging when I was growing up: Please don't hit me, please love me, please look at me as a person. Now I won't beg anybody for anything.

Ten years ago, I used to fish, crab trap and I made lots of money. I used to have a great big walk-in freezer where I'd have three turkeys at all times, half a pig and a quarter of beef. I used to walk out of the grocery with two carts full of food. All the neighbourhood kids would come over and I never said No to one. I was like a free drop-in centre. Today I don't have food, I don't have money. I feel like a part of me is being smothered. Can't share. Can't help.

I'm on a waiting list for BC Housing. I'm on a waiting list for Native housing. I'm on a waiting list for every housing imaginable. It has to be wheelchair accessible. Then BC public housing isn't exactly a nice environment, because people there are in such dire straits.

I don't have a telephone. I have a computer, because my son is in a wheelchair and that's his only access to the outside world. That's expensive. He's now just getting $175 instead of $481 a month, because they said he's not disabled.

Because you're Status Native, everybody thinks that your dental plan is taken care of. It's not. I probably need two root canals and have about eight cavities, but you're only allowed to have a certain amount done each year. You have x amount of dollars like everybody else to spend to get your teeth done. The thing is, you can't just walk in and get your teeth done. You have to walk in, get an appointment, and then they phone for approval, which can take

anywhere from three to six months. Meanwhile, you have a toothache.

Public financial assistance doesn't meet my needs. When I was younger, I knit and picked berries to survive. As I got older, I got to work and I was single and I had nobody else to worry about. It was the most liberating feeling that I could ever, ever feel! Then I had my children, I got on the Welfare system and that was a horrifying experience. I'd never wish that on any young mother. They act like God, like the money's coming out of their bank account. How about going after the deadbeat fathers as hard?

I get to have a roof over my head. That's it. It's not enough to have a telephone. It's not enough to buy one bra, never mind three pairs of underwear. Not for a job interview. I'm in the hole. I have two bank accounts, both in the minus. I have to walk everywhere. My Welfare cheque that I got today is already gone. It's direct deposit, but I already owe money for last month's food.

If I had a truck, and if I had gas, and if I had a boat, I'd go fishing, I'd go hunting, I'd get my own food. I'd like to grow my own vegetables and have my own little pig, my own little cow and my own chickens.

Being on BC Benefits is very degrading. I feel like a poodle, on show in a circus ring. Granted I'm not as well groomed. You have to jump through this and you have to land in that circle and you have to look pretty while you're doing it. You're not allowed to show emotion, you're not allowed to feel frustration. You're supposed to be, Oh so happy, Oh so grateful to get it. It's sickening. It makes me feel ill.

You're treated like you're 4 years old and they send your rent direct. You don't have the privilege of your landlord not knowing. That's really insulting to a lot of people. You have to fight to have it deposited into your bank account so you can have enough pride in being able to pay it yourself.

To help me find work? Make sure I don't have to worry about my rent. Give me $500 worth of food. Take care of my son so I can go look for work and not worry about whether he slipped and fell in the bathroom, to be able to know that he's fine. Get me a wheelchair-accessible house, so he can take care of himself.

If I want to kill myself, I know how to do it. I struggle with myself sometimes, like an everyday thing. I want to, I don't want to, I want to, I don't want to. What pulls me back? I don't know. That I might make a difference to somebody? I'd like to create my own little paradise, a piece of land where I can build a nice hotel. I'm not going to hire the people who've always had a job. I want somebody who hasn't been able to get a job for the last ten years and who wants one, so desperately. Then I'll have somebody who drives to pick up all my workers. If you can do it for tree spacers, why can't you do it for anybody else? Why can't you do it for women who want to work?

I'm hiding right now in this little place. I'm trying to gather my energy to go out in the world and say:
"OK, here I am again! Let's try it again. One more time. Let's get it right people!"
I think I'm so stupid sometimes, seriously, because I go out there and try again. I really, honestly think that I'm going to find someone who's going to help. It won't go away. *I just believe.*

Tatum

Method: Interview

I never had a mom and dad. I grew up with my grandparents, the youngest of many children, and seeing a lot of bad stuff - violence, alcohol abuse, sexual abuse. I experienced it, I lived it, all my childhood.

———

I was sexually molested by an uncle in my own home. Going to school was horrible. There was abuse going down on the bus and in the school all the time, so I was always sick when I was a little kid; something about not eating. People would start this abuse and I would crawl under the seats and go sit behind the bus driver, waiting to get off the bus. We travelled from the reserve to town, so it was quite a commute.

Nobody ever believed me. When I had my third child — a little girl — I just went nuts. I couldn't eat, I couldn't sleep, I couldn't do anything. My abuser was in my dreams, hurting my daughter. So then I came out, I talked about it to counsellors, I got help in the white society. When I talked about it to the family, I got disowned for two years.

I'd moved to town off the reserve and some friends were phoning and talking about him doing this, him doing that — the bus driver, this uncle that molested me. I was trying not to get involved. I said, It's not my problem. But I got sick from it. I just couldn't handle it.

Everybody in the reserve I've ever said things to — I tried to discuss sexual abuse, tried to discuss the violence — they'd say: 'It happened to me; it's going to happen to you; there's nothing you can do about it; it's going to continue; you can't stop it'.

I've heard this so many times in my life. I just could not comprehend it. I thought, No! Not in my head! Why do you people just gossip about it?! You have to DO something.

So I was the one who did it. Nobody else. I phoned the chief: "I'm going to inform all those parents what their rights are, if you don't get that bus driver out of there NOW." He did nothing. I threatened another time: "I'm going to come down there and tell ___ everything I know about women's rights." Nope. Finally: "I'm going to a lawyer."

I sued the uncle, the bus driver. They hired him back the following year.

My mom disowned me. That was really hurtful. That was my only family. It was devastating, to be brought up to be this proud little Indian and then disowned. She wanted everything back, my Indian jewellery, my Indian shawl. I said, "No, I have Indian kids to give them to. You gave them to me. They're mine." It was pretty harsh.

Two years went by and my family had a big Indian potlatch on the reserve; and of course I heard about it. My dad used to say: When it's our family, you don't have to be invited. So I went. My mom just hugged me and that was kind of the end of it.

Now when I go back, some of those children just love me! Their parents can't stand me. The children get it. That keeps me going. If I saved one kid, I don't care what anybody else thinks. One child's life is going to be better than mine.

———

I've been homeless twice, with three children, with a spouse. I know all about being homeless. I'm not with my spouse now. It's still difficult with some issues, but it makes a world of difference in our emotional state.

We've always had to just barely make it, even through nine years of ice hockey. How did I do that?! My family grew up in ___ and my father was a hockey coach in his day. That helped. Also my kids were such good players that some of the committees, the other hockey clubs, would pay for them to stay another year. So we did get a lot of assistance, but that doesn't mean they gave me gas or money to feed them on the weekends when they had to go out of town! That almost happened every weekend. With three kids. It was hard. It feels good, though, that I accomplished that for them.

There's never enough money. I only get $270 from Welfare, to live off all month. That has to pay my phone, my hydro and our food. I have kids that eat. We're always out of milk. I'm always telling the kids that we have to go shopping today to buy necessities — milk, eggs, bread. Never mind the band aids! My daughter won a first aid kit at a hockey tournament, so we had band aids for a short while. They're never on my necessities list. And coffee! What does that taste like?

I walk, I bus, I don't have a licence. I'm just about __ years old and never had a licence, because I can't afford even that. The most frustrating part is I could never watch the kids' hockey games out of town. I'd be stuck at home alone, wondering if they're winning and how much fun they're having. Now one of my children has started working. I can't get him to work and the buses are too late for his shift, so he has to walk. It's devastating.

I don't have a telephone because I have an outstanding bill. So I went and got more of an outstanding bill with this stupid cell phone. How am I going to get a job if I don't have a phone?

I never eat, because there's never enough food. I drink water and have fish sandwiches. My family fishes; I have to go to the reserve and prepare it. They give me the jars, because I can't afford jars and lids and sealing. When I'm fortunate enough to go to the reserve to get the fish done, I eat that all the time. And onions. That's all I buy for myself is a bag of onions. I have my jar of mayonnaise and fish sandwiches.

I don't have my own room. I have a boy and a girl at home, so they can't share rooms. I have to sleep on the couch. I never seem to have a good rest. My things are piled into a box in a cubby-hole, all wrinkled and ugly. That really bugs me. I need my own space. I really need my own space.

I'm always worried about hydro being cut off. My whole life it's been like that. I'm scared to cook or do something too long. I just really watch it.

My kids have supported us. My Band gives the children incentive money. Since Grade 1, I've been borrowing money from my oldest son to pay my bills and feed us, to get the phone back... Now he's probably scared to work and thinking, Where's my money going to go?

Do you know how that makes me feel? I would feel so much better to have an income, to sign my own cheque and be able to say, 'This is what you're allowed to spend this month and you deserve it'. Because they're really good kids, considering what we've been through.

I don't like handouts. I feel so much better when I work for it. Before I left the reserve, for three or four months I did work: work, work, work, work. Anything I could do, I would do it. I don't know how many cheques I piled up, but I bought a brand new vacuum cleaner for $300, I bought a car for $750, and I bought car insurance. And it felt good. All that was mine.

I'm a pretty happy and easy-going person, but right now I'm really angry. I don't like feeling like this. Some days, especially these days, I wake up feeling so bitter about this life. I've not accomplished anything. Ahhh. When I'm alone, I feel so unworthy of anything. When I laugh a little too hard I think, What am I doing?! I'm so scared to have a little bit of happiness. I really am.

I'm absolutely shocked I'm going to be turning __ years old. I thought I'd be dead by now. All my life, I used to think, I'm only here because they get money for having me. Turning __, that's one of the hardest things right now, with trying to change and get better. I have no idea what I want to do. Or be.

I went to International Women's Day. I didn't know there was such a thing, but I attended it this last year. I never felt so much pride in being a woman until that day. Then I started learning a little bit here and there about self-care. I'm still not quite there completely, but I see that's what I need. I was so emotional that night! I remember thinking, All I need is recognition. That would make a world of difference in my life.

Our talk about food really clicked in my mind yesterday. I kept thinking, Oh my goodness, no wonder I can't think and learn and all this! I never eat right! I had this big roast that my boyfriend cooked and left in the fridge — this great big honking roast! So I cut it all up, nuked it in the oven, put what I had in the fridge that he'd also left — celery, broccoli and cauliflower. I just threw it all in a burrito with sour cream and salsa.

After that I felt so good. I read 'til 11 o'clock. I soaked it in. I was getting it. So I thought, Hol-y! No wonder I've not been able to do stuff!

I used to wear extra large sweatshirts, cover myself constantly. Didn't matter how hot I was, I was hiding myself. If I'm upset or feeling really insecure, I still do that, but I try really hard not to. At Trade School and Horizons, they gave me dressy clothes. So now I've got nice dresses and some nice clothes to wear - free hairdos too. Never had hairdos!

I really enjoy waking up in the morning and getting dressed up nice. It makes a whole difference to my wellbeing throughout that day. I've learnt that I need to get a job in the morning hours. I want a routine: shower, get dressed, go to work. That's real important to me that it work out that way.

I'm physically fit, but since my last child was born I've had troubles. Got some kind of bad bleeding problem that goes on for months and months and months. It's been really bad these past four or six years. It doesn't stop; it's just constant, sore. That's why I'm scared to eat. The doctors don't seem to know. I'm sick and tired of going to them. They tell me nothing's wrong. Well, obviously, something's not right!

I lived in Vancouver when I was 19, 20, 21, or whatever. My whole life, I think that's what's a live and so burning anger. We lost our language and every other culture is out there yakking their language — on public buses and on public streets. Oooh, that used to burn me in Vancouver when I was young! I used to be so angry when I heard another nationality's voice in their own language. I think I still am. Then I have to be a Canadian citizen and you're telling me I have to know French?!?!

I never felt discrimination until I had this ex in my life. The ex was paying attention to the kids' homework, I guess, and one day he took my kid to school in town. I went with him the following day. He was really, really angry. Well, when I walked into that school with this Indian, I felt it. Renting in Victoria as well. There was so much discrimination. They would give the place to me when he was working. I'd want to make sure that he would be comfortable with it too, so I'd say, I'll be back at 6 o'clock. Then I'd bring my Indian husband. BAM! We don't have a place anymore. Two hours ago I had it! No problem, no question. Then they see this Indian... He was in work clothes and everything!

My ex uses the kids. We have three together and I always had the two — my daughter lived with him for a short while —, but he's always claimed he's had all three children. He just uses them for their money. These kids get nothing! He's an alcoholic, a drug abuser. I'm always feeding them. When I moved here and went to the food bank, the lady was stunned that I even existed. For two years, he'd been claiming he had three children.

It's sad for the kids. These beautiful kids that he's ruining... I think my eldest is getting it. Actually, I think my other son is too. He is very abusive to me, just like the dad has been. That's why he doesn't live with me. He got a job. I'm so worried about him working, because he's just going to have booze and more drugs and more bad things — but he's buying things! "It's getting boring drinking," he said.

He had a girlfriend a couple of summers ago. I was always afraid he was going to hit her. One day we went walking and he said something to the effect, "When somebody hits me is that abusive too?" This girl was abusing him — and he was walking away! I burst into tears: "Anybody who hits anybody is being abusive and you could be charging her for that. I thank you so much for walking away. The real strong man is the one who walks away and does not hit, son. So now you are a man."

———

For the future I would like a couple of things. I would like a great big humongous house for the Elders to live in and a location in this home for a daycare facility. I remember my grandpa just loved kids and he became a kid again. I always think that if you're a kid at heart, you're never going to grow old and wither away. So that's what the Elders need. That would be one goal.

Another thing I want to do is a Horizons for men. The more I'm growing, the more avenues open up. I sure would like to see kids get help. I'm interested in healing people. I want to educate Indians about what their rights are and how to go about getting what they need.

For myself, I want daily fulfillment, love and happiness.

Vanessa

Method: Interview

It was my first week in town and I was flipping through the paper. I saw a picture of my father-in-law giving a large donation to a local charity. I thought: 'Isn't that typical? Here I am starving and eating at the same place all winter and his family owes me spousal maintenance and took the houses from me'.

Right beneath the picture was the article about this project.

———

I grew up in Victoria, the middle child of a middle-class family. I spent a lot of time with my grandparents, who were extremely wealthy. I was a very outgoing kid: into every sport and wanting to do and see everything. I was a Candy Striper and would pick daffodils and take them down to the hospital; the bright yellow would brighten up the room. I enjoyed visiting elderly people in the neighbourhood and hearing their stories. I was a competitive gymnast and taught the younger kids. I never had a spare moment and always made the Honour Roll at the school I attended.

My family would fight a lot about religion — my father was Catholic and my mother was Anglican —, so being one of those get-on-top-of-it kind of people, I started checking into it myself. I was eight or nine when I began reading the Bible. I didn't understand a bloody word of it. When I was 14, my mother bought me a Special Edition Bible. I slowly plugged my way through it, still not understanding much. I had a hard time getting past the, 'And blah-blah begot blah-blah'. I started at Revelations and worked my way back instead.

I don't know if there's such a thing as God, but I use the Bible as a guide on how to think. It's all about the power of positive thinking: loving your enemies and treating people as you would like them to treat you. If you follow that, it works. You don't hold grudges, you don't feel jealous, you don't feel envy. My mom called me naïve and worried that people would walk all over me because of this.

When I thought about my future, one thing was clear: I didn't want to grow up and serve some man. I didn't want to get married. My mom stayed home all the time and she did *everything*. There was no freakin' way in hell I was staying home 'til 5 o'clock and making

Vanessa

sure someone's dinner was warm. I didn't want to be a servant. I worried and fretted about this. Then, when I did grow up, that's what I became. For years.

That's the biggest thing that bothers me about society: It beats your spirit out of you. You grow up with dreams. Then because you're a woman, you're expected to put them aside. My dreams were to be a doctor. When I was nine, I read *The Intern* by Dr. X and wrote my first report on the different types of brain cancers. I was obsessed with the medical world and finding cures. My dad said: 'Oh you'll probably grow up and make a good little nurse'. I did.

When I was 15, I became pregnant, but miscarried. Ever since, my whole focus was: 'Find an intelligent man, get pregnant and make sure that he's not in the picture anymore'.

At 17, I had a daughter. I knew I would have more children, but I still didn't want a man in the picture. Sure, I recognized the importance of two parents and I never stopped my daughter's father from seeing her, but I thought, What's wrong with having a man around for his child, but not for me? I did not want to be a wife; that's what it boiled down to. I could accept the notion of 'fatherhood', but not 'husband'.

My daughter and I were happy, even when we had no money. We did end up on Income Assistance for awhile. The father was ordered to pay $300/month child support, but I was getting only $50/month.

I became pregnant again and was engaged to the father, a very gentle, kind and loving person. Our relationship ended when I was still unable to get married.

As a young single mom, I got 'the look' from people. For a short period of time, I was on Welfare, but raising children on Welfare wasn't my goal. I found an incredible stigma against single or divorced women, even from my own father when I later got divorced: 'Why would you want to leave your husband? He gives you everything'. Well, yeah, including bruises all over my body. Nobody understood. I lost the kids in the divorce, I lost all the property, everything that we were apparently working for together.

It's not about traditional roles. I'm afraid that even my current partner, who I chose because of shared beliefs, will take a part of me away. That's happened throughout my life. I've wanted things and society has said, 'No, no, you're a girl; girls don't do that; girls don't think like that'. Stomp, stomp, stomp, stomp – until finally I got married. I cooked dinner every night and said 'No I won't go out', 'Yes I'll do that'. I lived under the rule, like millions of other women.

I was 20 when I had my second child and still living on my own. My son was 6 months old when I met my future husband. I'd already begun to feel the guilt of bringing these children into the world and seeing my son's father drive off and never come back. My daughter's dad would say, 'I'll be there Saturday'. She'd be all dressed up, waiting at the window and he wouldn't show up. And the poverty. Although I felt totally happy with my life, what about them? What had I done? I felt so much guilt that when I met ___, I thought maybe it was time.

I lived with him for four years before we got married. We had three children together. The years before we married were good, but we argued a lot. I was still quite feisty and wanting to live my own way, and he was quite controlling and determined to put a stop to that. He never wanted me to have company. He smoked pot and the house always smelt like it, so I never had anybody over. Did I get into the pot? Oh, God, no! I was dead against it. I threatened to leave him if he smoked around the kids.

We had lots of money. He worked for his father's company. It turned out he was also selling drugs, so he had a very good income. He owned three houses; two were rented out. The kids were well taken care of, but there were times when my husband wouldn't give me money for so long that we might not even have toilet paper. He'd never let me drive the family vehicle. If there was an emergency, I had to call him. If he didn't think it was an emergency, we waited. Even if I needed milk, I had to wait for him to come home. I felt trapped and I felt isolated.

He left me the first time six weeks into my first year of University. We'd been together for seven years when I began studying nursing. He didn't like that. There was a lot of homework and class preparation. I'd been extremely ill in ICU and had had some heavy duty health problems that year. It was a lot of stress on everybody. I was a horrible nag, too, because he wouldn't stop people coming over to buy little bags of pot. Then he started running grow houses. When I found pot plants in our house, *that was it*. I threw them down the stairs. For that, he beat the crap out of me and was charged with assault. The charge was stayed. Everything went nasty and bitter.

He went to Alberta for two years and I filed for divorce. It didn't go through; he hadn't left an address and he couldn't be found for the papers to be served. After a few months, he began sending money. With that, my student loan and me working long hours, the kids and I had everything we needed.

When he came back, I'd done a couple of years of school, had been on my own and was happier than ever. After his return, I became increasingly unhappy. I used to say to my mom, 'It feels like he actually reaches in and takes my energy out'. But the kids were ecstatic, so I thought I'd better try to make this work.

My husband revealed a few months later that he was gay and had been with other men.

He filed for divorce in 2000 and he got everything: the furniture, the vehicle, the dishes. Everything. *Everything*. Our lawyers wanted to settle by agreement and my lawyer didn't properly represent me. Under the agreement, we got joint custody, an order which my husband breached.

For a year, I didn't get to see or speak to the kids who were living with him. I should have had them 3-1/2 days a week, but he refused to let me see them. He didn't pay his child support. My lawyer refused to go to court. Having just come out of a severely abusive relationship, I was too tired to fight. As I said before, it's like society stomps the personality right out of you.

My lawyer said I had to give my husband the other three children for weekends. When they would go, sometimes it would be three or four days before I could even get through to anybody on the phone. He never returned them. In 2001, he took one of the children away from me. He tried everything to hurt me. He'd taken all the money; he'd depleted my child support so there wasn't enough money for rent. The place where we lived had no heat and it was unsanitary. He offered to babysit but would always arrive just *a bit too late* so that I would be late for work. He charged me with mental instability and criticized everything I did. He'd come and visit, then take off with my son and I would be frantically calling, trying to find out where they were. One time it was for three weeks and when I finally found them, my son was angry and said: 'Why didn't you come and get me, Mom'?

In March 2003, I ended up in Emergency. I'd had a grand mal seizure on the street. While I was in hospital, my dad visited and told me: 'Social Services asked us to watch the children while you were sick, but we had to go to Las Vegas, so they gave them to your husband'. I said to myself: 'No thinking, thinking hurts'. I went completely weak.

That was that. I saw the kids maybe five times over the course of a year and I've gone to court many, many times.

When the kids first left, I never got out of bed. I couldn't work. I couldn't think. It's pretty lonely trying to get used to a house without kids in it. That never happens. I'll never get used to waking up without them.

Last Fall, I obtained Income Assistance. It's hard to get well if you have no money and it's a lot of work being poor. You are so busy trying to get food. I couldn't figure out how to eat healthy with no money and on the food they give out at the food bank. I've learned this slowly. You can't get *enough* food, but you can get healthy food, which means never having anything else. You have to be up at 8 o'clock or else you're going to miss the food hampers. If you're sick on the day they give them out, you have to wait a week.

Living below the poverty line is like living on another planet. I don't go to the grocery store; I get my food at the food bank. I can't afford breakfast foods or the odd bagel, so my dinners are extremely important. I used to be a vegetarian, but I can't afford fresh vegetables. Now I have to eat fish and chicken. Occasionally I eat beef. I need the protein so badly. I wish I got cheese but no one gives it out. You can't get fresh milk products.

Ironically, I'm probably more physically fit than I have been in a long time. I walk everywhere because I have to. I see the world so totally differently. I don't value money anymore. I value relationships. I enjoy simple things more. Before, my husband would say to me: 'You'd give your neighbour your last loaf of bread and leave yourself with nothing'. I knew that mothers had a hard time getting formula. I didn't know what being in poverty felt like – you are a different race, you live a different life, even from people who have just enough money to get by. You don't go to the dentist and if you're tooth falls out, too damn bad. You can be so hungry at times that your stomach hurts. You don't cry about it or feel sorry for yourself anymore, because that's your reality.

I think the general population goes around with their eyes closed. For example, I saw my dad recently for the first time in over a year. When I was leaving, he offered me $20. I told him, 'That's not why I wanted to see you.' You don't need money to survive as much as you need community and human connection. My dad doesn't understand. He said to me the other day, 'Well if you're sick, just rest' – yeah, well, I've got to go do my laundry in the bathtub, so I'll just pass on that. My family are just clueless and they don't want to know what it's like.

I've been accepted into the nursing refresher program but still need to get the funding. I'm now allowed to see the kids — whenever I want, if I give enough notice. This is for eight months, until I'm out of school. So my future looks excellent, but it was hard work getting here. I can't see it going bad either way, whether I get the funding to take the course or if I pay for it myself through working part-time.

I don't see myself as living in poverty very much longer and within a year, I should be as happy as a clam, happier than I ever was before. I'll have my kids back.

I've had a really great learning experience. Probably everybody should spend a year of their life living in extreme poverty. No longer than a year. Otherwise, you may not be able to claw your way out of it.

Waneta

Method: Interview

My mother was Coast Salish. She had three children: me, my sister who is four years older and my brother who is two years younger. My mother had my sister with a man she later married; she found out afterwards he was gay. She met my father in Victoria. I don't know who my father is. As far as I know he's Blackfoot. Once I was conceived, she hitchhiked to Alberta. A woman answered the door. Apparently, he had a wife and children already. My mother met a non-Native man next. He was a biker and into drinking, drugs and partying. They had quite a wild relationship. My younger brother was born with him. So there's three of us with the same mother, different fathers.

My mother settled in Victoria.

When I was 5 years old, she committed suicide in a motel room. My younger brother and I were present and were the ones who actually found her. We remember that night like it was yesterday. We found her in the bathroom. There were no adults around. We remember playing with her rope.

My older sister's father took her to live with him. My grandfather took me. My younger brother went to live with his father. So the three of us were separated immediately after my mother's death. Then there's this big four-year blackness, where I don't remember anything. Suddenly I'm 9 years old, with my grandfather and I've had no connection with my sister or brother.

My grandfather was a fisherman and always in and out of the home. His partner would beat me, hit me, kick me, and make me do a lot of chores. I was like a little slave. I slept in a crib in a corner of the same room where my grandparents and uncle slept. I remember being in my room a lot. I was only allowed to come out to eat and to go outside at certain times. And to go to school.

I remember in Grade 4 being kept back at school and missing the bus. I had to walk home. I was almost home and this guy pulled up behind me and tried to get me into his car. He said, 'Your daddy told me to come and pick you up'. I looked at him, shook my head and said, 'No, I don't have a daddy'. Then I ran home. I told them, but by the time they had gone to look, he had left. I was told I was a liar. They didn't believe me.

There were different times in that house that I was abused by another of my aunts. One time, she whipped me off a chair and started throwing me around the room. I went flying into the corner of the TV. I have a big scar on my head. She tried to clean it up and swore to me that if I told anybody, I would get worse. A few days later, I was with one of my uncles and it started bleeding. He asked what had happened. I told him that I fell. That's something I've recently begun to deal with through WAVAW.

Different kinds of abuse went on in the home at different times. One of the uncles that lived in the home started sexually abusing me. I didn't know that it was wrong. We would go fishing and then he would get on top of me and stuff. He'd make me lay there. I didn't know. All of us slept in the same room as my grandfather and his partner. Seeing him on her, I thought it was something that you did. My uncle was doing that to me at the creek, when I was nine, and I thought it was what you had to do. I've never told any of the family members. He told me not to tell anybody, of course. I had all these secrets. All these adults in my life were telling me, 'Don't tell, Don't tell'.

At different times when my grandfather and his partner were gone, other guys were at the house and they were doing the same things to my older aunts. I was told to stay in the room and not come out. Being in my room and cleaning up, that was my life. And school.

On my birthday, my grandfather was killed in a car accident. After he died, I went to live with my aunt and uncle up-Island. They had four children and brought me up from the age of nine. I consider them my mother and father. They worked full-time and really tried hard to do things with us, bring us places and buy us all our needs. There was affection; they would tell me they loved me and give me hugs. A few years later, my mother started to drink and became verbally and physically abusive to us and very strict.

I was about 13 when my biological sister reunited with me. She visited us off and on for about a year. She took her life when she was 18. She also hung herself in Victoria. Six months later I was reunited with my brother. My mom got court access to him, but he stayed with us only for six or seven months. He told his social worker about the abuse that was going on in the home and he was removed to another foster home.

I was probably about 14 or 15 when my adoption into my family went through. I changed my name and changed Bands. I was happy with that.

When I was 19, I got into partying and met my boyfriend, who is not Native. That created a lot of anger with my relatives. They were really hard on me, and my mother and I grew further apart. But I continued with my boyfriend, who is now my partner in life.

When I lived with my boyfriend, we lived in a hotel above a bar. From there, I started working and earning my own money. I worked at that first job for three years. I also volunteered at the local Boys & Girls Club and got a job as the after-school program coordinator. I juggled both jobs, and for extra money would go fishing on the weekends. I was making a lot of money, but also partying in my off-time. I also managed to squeeze in my ECE[9] through home-schooling, which took me two years to complete.

With my ECE, I applied at a Safe Home in Vancouver. I got hired right away. It was double the pay I'd been making. The only downside was that I was away from home for four days at a time. My partner still lived on the Island and so it was a strain on our relationship. I did that job for six years.

In 1999, I had a miscarriage, went into depression and had to go off work for a couple of months.

In 2000, I became pregnant again. Until I was five months' pregnant, I commuted back and forth between Vancouver and the Island. My stress level went back up, and I developed high blood pressure which required medication. I had to leave work and stay at home.

My son was born in December. The partying stopped for me, but not for my partner. I left my partner when my son was 5 months old and moved into my uncle's home. My partner joined us a couple of months later. By this time, my Employment Insurance had run out and I had to go on Social Assistance. That meant scrimping and scraping to get by and surrendering my car. I cooked and cleaned, and did meal preparation in return for rent.

We moved into an apartment for about eight months. We really needed our own home because we had our two dogs. That was our downfall when we were looking for rental places; they wouldn't accept the dogs. We gave one dog to friends in another town. We had the other at a friend's in town; that didn't work out and we had to give him up. The dogs were like our babies. We'd raised them since they were 6 weeks old and we carried them everywhere with

---

[9] Early Childhood Education certificate.

us. It was heartbreaking to take one to the SPCA. He was my dog. I couldn't believe that I'd actually got rid of him.

So I got through that stage. We turned to looking for a new place and everywhere we looked, I ran into people who were prejudiced or had lots of attitude. It was getting frustrating. Anybody who has a status card can apply for Native low income housing. So that's what I did and it has helped me a lot. We're still there, in the same townhouse.

I was determined to get work, so I took all these little courses that Social Services was offering and sent my resume out all over the place. People would say they were interested in me, but then I would get there and I wasn't able to get employed. I have a lot of experience, but I don't have a Bachelor's or a Master's degree. I was finding that quite a bit and was getting frustrated.

I've always had a struggle with school, was put in special classes and made fun of because I was Native. I still struggle with Math and English. I'm not sure how I got to where I am, because now I am a student at Malaspina taking First Nations Child & Youth Care.

I started school last September and once I applied for that course I was cut off Welfare. They would not cover a two-year diploma program and told me to apply for a student loan. I did and my application was accepted. I've also been approved for a Band living allowance.

In April I finished my first year of school and over the summer I did three part-time jobs. My boyfriend cut back his hours so he could stay home with our son, who had been acting out. That's why we pulled him out of daycare in April. His behaviour did a turnaround once Daddy was home.

Now things are looking up and I'm getting ready to go back to school in September. It's been very busy for me and I've been exhausted, but I'm determined to get this one year done and am thinking about doing third and fourth year.

I try to go every week for counselling. I took the life skills program and with it, began my healing. I understand why I act the way I do. I'm trying to break the family cycle of abuse.

My diet has become healthier over the past while. We try to stay within the four food groups, cut out the junk food and eat more vegetables. I get my food at the local grocery store. I get fish, deer meat and clams through my brother. Sometimes I have to go to the food bank and I also get a Christmas food hamper. I use those resources when we really need them. I also participate in the Good Food Box program.

I have a phone and a computer. I have a vehicle, which is a big bonus. If my partner takes the vehicle, we bus it.

My relationship with my family is distant. My focus is my own family now. I also have family support in the Valley and Victoria that I go to. I have a handful of close, supportive friends and I'm happy with that.

Ten years ago I was into the party life and physically I'd say I was a 5 on a scale of 1 to 10. Now I'm a 7.5. I do have high blood pressure and am on medication for that.

My state of mind has changed. It's been up and down. I've had some stressful days, and days when I've just wanted to cry and I don't know where that's coming from. I have a counsellor through WAVAW and she has been helping me a great deal. I have not seen a Mental Health professional. There is still that big blackness. I'm afraid of what will come up and I'm not sure if I'm ready to deal with it.

I'm actually meeting my needs now. I'm setting boundaries and not caretaking the whole family anymore. I have to learn how to look after my own needs, which are always met last. I am working on developing some hobbies. I have no hobbies, but when I was younger I liked to paint and do crafty things. I like to read too. I like to listen to music. I spent a lot of time with my dogs before, going out for walks and taking them to the bush.

Basically my life is home, school and work. I tried to get involved in a fitness program but there was no motivation to keep going. I need to go to a place where there is a lot of support. So my goal is to try to get myself involved in a fitness activity again and to walk more.

My income has gone up and down, from having no children and good pay, to having a child and struggling with EI after having a paycheque. When I went on Assistance it was even more of a struggle. It was very stressful. I was afraid to ask for help and had to borrow things. I went to the thrift stores often. I remember wondering how people could survive on it, including myself.

I'm still with my partner. My partner has been very supportive of me and we've been together since '89. We've had a lot of bumps in the road. He has stayed by my side and I have stayed by his side. I have been very supportive of him. He is from an alcoholic background. He does still drink but it isn't as bad as it was before. Since he's had the connection with our son, he's slowed down a lot.

He's more respectful and he's more helpful around the house. Our relationship has actually been quite good and getting a lot stronger. I would like him also to get trained for a real job and be a role model for his son.

My own focus is on school now and whether I want to be a child and youth care worker or a social worker. My goal is to finish my education and buy our own home, where we could have a dog again. I want our son to see both of his parents having a good job and being role models and breaking the cycle of dysfunction.

Once I have finished my Diploma, I intend to work full-time on the Island. I would like to help my People. I would like to continue to educate my son. And I would like to help those who are in need.

Project Reports

Phase 1 - The Issues

We will not give you statistics. We will not say how many of us are students, retired, single mothers, living alone or living with a spouse, working or on government assistance. We will say that we have all those covered. We will not give our ages, since age is irrelevant to who we are.

Because we want you to read all our stories, we will provide no references to indicate from which stories the quotations were taken. Each story is quoted at least once.

This report details the issues that feature dominantly in our stories. Our second report, Phase 2 — The Recommendations, contains our suggestions for preventing and remedying those issues.

Our report has three major divisions: i) **Predictors** are conditions which have tended to forecast our future poverty; we have identified two broad long-term and one short-term or immediate predictors. ii) **Primary effects** are caused by the immediate or **primary conditions** of poverty; iii) **Secondary conditions** are causing **secondary effects**. The latter are sometimes increases in the magnitude of the primary effects or are new effects. The diagram on the following page illustrates the relations among predictors, primary and secondary conditions and primary and secondary effects.

Policies of Exclusion, Poverty & Health

Long-term predictors
(Conditions in earlier life)

Short-term predictors

Poverty = Income below LICO

Primary	Conditions of Poverty	Secondary
a, b, c, d, e, ...	Primary conditions are material situations.	i, ii, iii, iv, v, ...
	Secondary conditions tend to be social conditions.	

Primary	Effects of conditions	Secondary
1, 2, 3, 4, 5, ...	Primary effects due to primary conditions.	1, 2, 4, 5, p, q, ...
	Secondary effects due to secondary conditions. The conditions can enhance primary effects and introduce new effects.	

TIME →

Long-term Predictors

We discovered two major long-term predictors of future poverty in our stories: 1) childhood trauma, and 2) gender discrimination and pressures to conform.

The #1 predictor of future poverty was overwhelmingly an event, more often a course of events, that traumatized us during childhood. The events mentioned in the greatest number of our stories were abuse, neglect, or exploitation by a guardian or family member. Fourteen of us report having had experiences of this sort. In several cases of abuse, other family members or the community knew about it and did nothing, which increased our isolation and furthered our pain.

A few stories suggest childhood exploitation. As little girls, we were held responsible for maintaining the household and caring for our siblings or parents, or we lived an underground existence as immigrant children. Far too many of us experienced neglect and lack of love or affection. We felt worthless, devalued, our identity threatened: "I felt like a non-person."

Sexual assault and exploitation by a non-guardian feature in a number of our stories. This appears in some of the same stories that report family abuse, but also in others. Rape during the teen years is mentioned several times.

In several cases, we escaped to the streets, only to be further abused or exploited: "I usually traded sex for somewhere to live... When you're 14, 15 years old, there are a lot of quasi pedophiles who don't actually want children, but don't want grownups either."

The breaking up of the family by divorce or death was another condition causing us anguish. The extent to which we were affected by parental breakup was due largely to how our custodial parent managed the change and whether both parents remained in our lives. In some cases, the loss or absence of a father stamped our future choices: "Almost all of my relationships have been with men 17 to 27 years older." Many parents did not manage the change well, turning instead to alcoholism or addiction and unhealthy relationships. Both created situations that threatened our young lives.

In two cases, there was parental suicide. One little girl found her mother's body.

The #2 predictor of future poverty was gender discrimination and pressures to conform. Many of us have been independent, outside-the-box thinkers for as long as we can remember: "I was pretty outgoing as a really young child. If I thought something was crap, I would say so. The first time my mom took out her stuff on me, I sat her down the next day and said, 'You got a little out of control'. Just had this rational discussion! I was 7... I'd love to be able to do that now. I just got worn down."

We have been inclined to challenge the status quo and traditional roles. Most of us encountered gender bias for the first time in our families. Others first experienced it while at school. Later, we met it in the workforce and when trying to obtain credit for loans and services: "I applied for a job as manager of a [non-local] candy store. The interviewer said he would never hire me; he'd just wanted to see 'what kind of woman thinks she can manage a candy store'."

We have been steered toward traditional roles when our dreams soared higher. The mother of one storyteller had ambitions of being a doctor. For her, the loss of her dream, coupled with other pressures, led to grief for her daughter. One of us shared that same dream: "When I was nine, I read *The Intern* by Dr. X and wrote my first report on the different types of brain cancers... My dad said: 'Oh you'll probably grow up and make a good little nurse'." Another storyteller wanted to go to university, but was steered to the nursing and secretarial (vocational) stream. Yet another wanted to enter the computer field. She also was steered to secretarial training.

We have been ridiculed by teachers and peers – and sometimes beaten – for being 'different', or for daring to question or challenge prevailing views: "Mostly quiet, when I did speak up I would speak the truth and that would upset people." School was rife with rules, some nonsensical, most inflexible. An A student asked for special consideration when her father was dying: "I'd been getting excellent marks and couldn't see myself writing tests. I went to the Principal, who knew my dad and knew the family. He said, 'We can't make any exceptions'. I went to each teacher. All except my English teacher refused... That was the end of school... [It] was like jail."

The educational system failed our independent thinkers in other ways: "The postgraduate process is another form of indoctrination, of learning to think and do in a prescribed way." Its gender bias is evident right to the top: "The very nature of academic study involves argument, with students expected to 'assert' a thesis or 'defend' a position. [It's] a battleground."

Two surprises

Childhood poverty — Not. In our stories, childhood poverty was not a long-term predictor for our present financial condition. Far more, it was a traumatic event in adult life, the handling of which was undermined by trauma during childhood.

Researchers sometimes argue that poverty itself traumatizes a child. Our experiences suggest otherwise. It's how a family handles poverty that matters: "My parents made it OK to be poor."

Also, childhood abuse is often associated with poverty conditions. Our stories oppose that too. While many of us are survivors of childhood abuse, all who are mothers have broken the cycle.

Education and literacy — Not. We are literate. Compared to the general population, our group has an unusually high number of women with above-average intelligence. 17 storytellers have one or more years post-secondary education; five have three or more years. As teenagers, we were determined to get our high school diploma, no matter what else was going on in our lives: "I always made it really clear that whatever deal I was in, I was going to go to school." This was the young girl who traded sex for a place to live.

Lack of education within our families provided the impetus to succeed: "Graduating was important, because no one else in the family had graduated."

Short-term Predictors

For a large majority of us, there was only one immediate predictor of coming poverty, a traumatic event during adulthood.

Abusive relationship/leaving an abusive relationship. Either being in, or exiting from an abusive relationship plunged many of us into poverty. If we'd previously had income, this was eroded through the marriage, or the family income wouldn't be accessible to us during the relationship. We, and sometimes our children, would live in poverty while our spouse did not. On breakup, we would have poor legal representation. In one case, our children were taken away. In other cases, there was no or little help in going after deadbeat dads. In a third case, assets were not divided equally; our spouse got everything, we got nothing.

Physical trauma. Two of us were in car accidents which led to some form of disability. With others, the erosion of our health due to disease led to permanent disability.

Past resurfaces. In at least three cases, a sudden emotional breakdown was triggered by the reappearance of family members who played roles in traumatizing us during childhood. In a fourth case, the past infected the present when one of us took our childhood abuser to court. The emotional turmoil of that process ended the marriage.

Sexual assault. One woman was raped while her children were in another room. Police would not pursue; she was not given medical attention. Another woman was assaulted by her boyfriend...

Not all of us are living in extreme poverty. Six storytellers live within reach of the poverty line or are on their way out of poverty: three of those have sources of funding not available to the rest; one is retired, has a supportive family, decent transportation and a mortgage-free home; another has just received funding for training that is likely to bring her a positive future; the sixth is beginning a warm, loving relationship that won't involve struggling to make ends meet. We're delighted for each and every one of them.

The remaining 15 women are living within, or within reach of, extreme poverty:

Extreme poverty is experienced by people whose incomes are thousands of dollars below the poverty line. This is that other line which Statistics Canada publishes annually, the one that marks the poverty gap. An income that low creates the following primary conditions:
- not having enough, or any, nutritious food
- not having a means of transportation, other than walking
- not having comfortable, safe, secure, or sanitary housing
- not having dental care
- not having extended medical care, including chiropractic and physiotherapy treatment
- not having a telephone
- not having adequate clothing and footwear
- not having ...

Primary Effects

Our stories expose the true cost of living in poverty: the erosion of human spirit and the failure of society to capitalize on human potential. As bleak as that may sound, there is room for hope.

Our stories make an important connection between economic factors and their socioeconomic consequences, not just for us, but for the communities in which we live. Perhaps by making these links so obvious, we may help those in government see the economic benefits of stamping out poverty. Government so often disregards social issues in favour of the economic. With respect to poverty, our stories show that the disconnect simply doesn't work.

We reveal two major direct effects of living in extreme poverty. First and foremost is the deterioration of our emotional wellbeing. Second is the deterioration of our physical wellbeing. While both might be brought together under the heading of 'Health', we think they are best treated separately for reasons that will become apparent.

1. Deterioration of emotional wellbeing

The most significant direct effect of our living in extreme poverty is the deterioration of our emotional wellbeing, or more broadly, our mental health. What is happening to us is frightening and dangerous. Our stories shocked even us. We'd been so busy trying to survive that we hadn't noticed our life-force draining away.

Our words give warning to ourselves and others: We are exhausted, depressed, angry and stressed. Half of us are suicidal.

Exhaustion. This dominates our lives, as becomes evident in the number of times we use words like 'exhaustion', 'tired', or 'worn out'. It's as though we can't think of anything else beyond our fatigue:

- I'm so, so tired... just enough to live, to be able to survive, to jockey all the things going on.
- I'm exhausted ... I'm just exhausted, because the thought of waking up and trying to live through another day the way we have been is overwhelming.
- How tired can I possibly be?! Sometimes I can't string a sentence together.

- I'm so tired of my needs not being met. I'm so tired of moving all the time.

In several cases, we see a link between exhaustion and the development of depression, despair and hopelessness.

Depression and despair. In more than half of our stories, we talk of feeling depressed and sad, in despair and of our hope dying; other stories allude to these states. Often our words appear within the same sentence or paragraph as references to exhaustion (see also 'Stress').

- I live on a razor's edge. Right now, just maintaining work and maintaining my health takes everything. It takes everything I've got.
- I've stopped trying to find an employer, since the repeated rejection has become more than I can bear. I avoid people for fear I'll start crying.
- In a project like this, how many women are ... so tired – and I don't mean sick and tired – I mean literally almost exhausted to death and hopeless to death from trying to struggle through one more day?

Anger and frustration. Most of us are frustrated and angry; others have gone beyond those, feeling rage. The presence of these emotions becomes obvious in the way we tell our stories. Some women have taken sarcasm to a fine art.

Stress. Given the primary conditions of poverty, we get no relief from stress. Even sleep is disturbed by it.

Thoughts of death. For many, suicidal thoughts are a daily fact of life. At least seven of us make this point explicitly. Others allude to it. Three more, after they completed their stories, shared with the interviewer that they'd had suicidal thoughts; either a cultural taboo prevented them from mentioning it in their stories or they feared that admission would somehow prompt the deed. (Talking helped.)

- If I didn't have these children and if I didn't have an ex-husband that the thought of him ever getting custody of [them] would kill me, I probably would have ended my life long ago. There's a point where you just can't keep doing it. It costs too much to live.
- My pets keep me alive a lot of times when I would just rather not do it anymore.

- I got so tired of being poor. I found it so stressful that I wanted to die.
- If I want to kill myself, I know how to do it. I struggle with myself sometimes, like an everyday thing.

For many, it becomes a logical argument: If I haven't the money to live, why continue the struggle? As survivors of childhood trauma, we fought messages that said we were worthless. Poverty feels as abusive, because it brings with it the same messages.

Challenges to self-esteem. Most of us struggle to maintain our self-esteem. That makes us angry. We try to counter poverty's onslaught, but it's hard:

- You're a case file, you're 'the client'. You're never 'this person'. Nobody would ever say to their supervisor: 'This person needs help'... So you cease to be.
- One person stands on one side of a counter 'qualifying' another person who stands on the other side of the counter.

On or off the system, we share many experiences. We feel "unequal in a lot of [our] friendships." We're boring. We "can't go out to play." Unthinkingly, our friends or family may pay for our meals or transportation. We appreciate their kindness, but: "I don't like anybody paying my way, unless I ask them. It takes away my choice."

Isolation. Sheer lack of money creates conditions of isolation and marginalization. It challenges the ability to participate socially, not just because we can't pay our way (as described in the above paragraph), but in ways one might not think of:

- Poverty keeps people away. I don't have a car or a phone. I can't entertain.
- I don't fit. Sometimes I just feel like I don't fit anywhere.
- The isolation ... [is] comparative to solitary confinement. I can't afford a babysitter. I can't afford the bus ... and I won't walk at night.
- I love making things and giving them away. It breaks my heart because I can't do it.
- I feel like a part of me is being smothered. Can't share. Can't help.
- I don't have the money to make phone calls... I haven't seen [my family] in three years.

2. Deterioration of physical wellbeing

Second to the deteriorating effects of extreme poverty on our emotional health, are those on our physical wellbeing.

Low energy. Low energy is caused by a number of factors, including lack of nutritious food, the requirements for maintaining emotional stability and the requirements for maintaining the physical endurance to keep moving.

Emotional demands reduce energy: Those of us struggling daily with suicidal thoughts talk of the energy needed to fight the temptation to give in.

Physical demands reduce energy: All of us are stressed and most are malnourished, which makes our energy stores already low. Most of us walk everywhere, since we haven't a vehicle and cannot afford transit fare.

Weight. Some of us have gained weight from being on the 'Welfare diet'. Three make the connection between weight gain and diabetes. A few of us are underweight because we don't eat enough. We see ourselves with only two choices: eat a high-carb diet or eat much less, but at least some nutritious, food.

We have described extreme poverty as producing certain primary or material conditions of deprivation. The items we are going without are fundamental to living in a modern society.

The major primary effects from living under such conditions are foremost, the deterioration of our emotional wellbeing. Second is the deterioration of our physical wellbeing. The conditions facing us are already bad, but then come conditions that can exacerbate our situation and so increase the deterioration of our health. We call these 'secondary conditions' or 'secondary causes' of secondary effects.

Most secondary conditions fall from government policies and programs (including partner programs). Others extend into the general community. We list these to raise awareness and increase understanding, not to impute blame.

Secondary Conditions & Effects

A number of systemic factors impede our ability to rise out of poverty. Other factors that were originally intended to help, instead further our slide. We've grouped these secondary conditions into five general categories:

- Policies, Programs and their Administration
- Health Services
- Food – Getting It and Special Diets
- Transportation and Communications
- Additional Factors

1. Policies, Programs and their Administration

By far the greatest challenges we face in getting out of poverty and recovering our health are government income assistance and employment policies and related partner programs. Our stories expose certain illogical criteria and regulations related to some of these services, and why they can harm women in poverty rather than help.

In the following, we make no distinction between the policies and programs of the federal and provincial governments. Due to the complexity of poverty, all levels of government, including municipal, will have to work together toward finding solutions. We can help. (See our report Phase 2 – The Recommendations.)

Self-employed and working poor. Self-employed women who live below the poverty line face tough challenges. We have higher employment expenses compared to people with regular jobs. There are no employee/employer contributions to Canada Pension Plan (CPP) or Employment Insurance (EI), no extended health coverage, no dental plan, no vacations, and so on. It's unlikely we have savings or RRSPs, so we'll retire into poverty too:

- I should have been contributing to Canada Pension, ... but with two kids to feed, I couldn't afford to think about my future.

- I am one of the working poor. The reward for that is more poorness. It's, 'Sorry lady, you did a really good job. You raised those kids. You were only on Welfare for eleven months. Good for you, good for you — here are your pennies'.

Everything we earn is spent on sustaining our lives and our source of income. If competition comes along and suddenly we find ourselves without work, there is no EI, because we haven't been able to pay into it.

Our self-employed storytellers can attest to how quickly the working poor or 'underemployed' can face homelessness. We try to prevent the slide by finding more contract or parttime work. Failing that, we try applying to government employment programs. That's where we can find ourselves blocked.

Access to employment programs. There are excellent government-funded programs out there (e.g., JobWave), but they are available only to people on EI and/or BC Benefits (Welfare or Income Assistance and Disability Benefits). The working poor and self-employed who also live below the poverty line do not have access to these programs, unless they pay the fee themselves.[1]

A case in point are the government-sponsored programs run by FutureCorp. Their purposes are to get people off BC Benefits and onto self-employment. Our stories outline some of the problems we encountered when trying to get help with self-employment:

- FutureCorp fee-waived (or fee-reduced or fee-postponed) programs are available only to people on BC Benefits or EI.
- Assuming someone is on BC Benefits, training and funding are provided only for new self-employment ventures. Ventures begun on one's own initiative previous to applying for help are not eligible.
- Only training obtained through FutureCorp is recognized; experience and previous training is not. One woman already took FutureCorp training which she paid for herself. She has been told she must retrain — subject to qualifying for Disability Benefits.

---

[1] There is a rumour that some programs have recently been, or are about to be implemented, that will be available free to people who aren't on the system. That would be wonderful. We have no proof of their existence, however.

- Someone in the loans business suggested that our entrepreneur, who has lots of experience and training but no equity, contact the Disability Resource Centre. In other words, apply for Disability Benefits: "That's a violation of my human rights, having to play a victim role... Whether or not [I have a disability] shouldn't be a basis and foundation for me getting funding."

The problems don't seem to be so much with FutureCorp as with government regulations that dictate who is eligible to receive their programs and what those programs may offer. That said, we do wonder about apparent lack of flexibility.

There are also excellent employment programs for students — if the students are under 30 years of age.

Dental care. Since the Spring 2002 BC budget, adults on Income Assistance (IA) get no dental coverage other than for emergency tooth extraction. Most of our working poor can't afford even that. Native women haven't got it much better.

- You can't just walk in and get your teeth done. You have to ... get an appointment and then they phone for approval, which can take anywhere from three to six months. Meanwhile, you have a toothache.
- One tooth was chipped three years ago and bites into my cheek, my gums are receding, some teeth are loose. I chew my food carefully to preserve what teeth I have left.

Employment Insurance. Our region's unemployment rate is 9.7%.[2] The chances of finding permanent employment, fulltime or parttime, are limited. Chances of finding temporary employment are better. If we land temporary jobs, we are unlikely to qualify for EI. Still, should we try collecting the money we paid into EI, we may receive a letter stating that "your sporadic employment history" does not qualify. We try so very hard to find and keep employment. Then we get a letter that dismisses the value of those efforts.

Employment expense and earnings exemption. In Spring 2002, the BC Liberal Government withdrew the $200 earnings exemption for Welfare recipients. Now, if someone receives money from whatever source, exactly that amount is deducted from her Welfare cheque. People on Disability Benefits are allowed a $400 earnings exemption. In both cases, there is no allowance for employment

---

[2] May 2001.

expenses, unless the recipient is self-employed under a recognized self-employment program. That takes us back to FutureCorp.

One of us has a parttime job that earns her $200/month. She has transportation costs.

Another woman has costs due to self-employment. For a short while she was collecting Welfare. Her self-employment costs were not considered, since she'd created her small business before, not after, requesting FutureCorp's help.

One woman is on Disability Benefits (DB). A housing subsidy is tied to her requiring those benefits. She works hard and is close to the $400 exemption. She has employment expenses. If she manages to build up a few more employment hours, she will exceed the $400, lose her DB and her subsidy.

All three women are financially punished for working, yet they want and need to work to feel good about themselves. Which do they choose? To have more money in their pockets or to do something to help boost their self-esteem and which could possibly move them toward full employment?

With respect to expenses, there is something called the 'Community Volunteer Supplement'[3]. It allows up to $100/month "for clothing, transportation and other expenses needed for a person in the family unit to participate in a community volunteer program." The Act, in other words, will pay for expenses for unpaid work but not for paid work. Few people receiving IA are made aware of this supplement; many would qualify.

Housing. A single person on Welfare receives $510/month. The legislation supposes that $325 is sufficient for shelter and that the remaining $185 is enough for everything else.

Because $325 a month cannot get anyone decent, self-contained housing that is within walking distance to shopping and services, it must be expected that single women will share accommodation with other people. There are two problems with this. First, few rental opportunities exist for as little as $325/month. Second, we are female; we do not feel safe living with strangers.

Another consideration is pets. Landlords that permit pets are hard to find, yet our stories reveal that the presence of a pet can be the only thing keeping a woman (most often single) alive. To expect her to give up her pet to find shelter is cruel, even dangerous.

Women needing inexpensive accommodation are vulnerable: "I got an apartment in an area that is populated by Welfare

---

[3] § 52 of the BC Employment and Assistance Act.

recipients and the working poor... The landlord suggested 'other methods' of paying rent."

The search for safe, secure and sanitary housing creates other challenges. We find ourselves moving a lot, because we are constantly trying to find better conditions. This gives the impression to potential employers, creditors and service providers that we are unreliable. Our single moms face an even worse situation: "You move a lot because you're trying to find safer, more sanitary housing... At the same time, the Ministry of Human Resources is telling you: 'You're moving around too much. You're not providing a stable home for your children. If you don't stop this, we're going to take them away'."

Children with special needs. Especially for special needs children, there is a lack of adequate daycare in the community.

Of the Disability Tax Benefit, one woman was denied it for her son because he "isn't sick enough yet." She was also denied a Fuel Tax Number (to help with transportation costs) because her son "isn't 16 years old yet." Another woman, whose child has the same illness, was denied similar assistance.

Then there's the foster care vs. home care issue. A foster home that has a child with special needs receives up to $1500/month, a regular home no more than $900.

Threats of removal of children. Our single mothers have undergone, and been threatened with, the removal of their children.

- "My son would get a lot more help if I wasn't here, a lot more help from the Government. They would have somebody else to help him... Other than me, somebody who's tired. They've told me so. But they expect me to abandon him first. The Government said that if I needed help and I couldn't deal with my stressful life as a single mother, they would take my children from me and put me somewhere where I could get help. They have tried twice to remove my children from my home because I needed help dealing with stress and all my financial burdens. The stress is simply for lack of funds."

Of course, should you move around a lot too... (see Housing).

A policy issue of a different sort would make one laugh if it weren't so humiliating: "Now at the schools they've got all these lunch Nazis that watch what the kids eat and report on you. Yeah, just what the world needs, lunch Nazis."

Policies of Exclusion, Poverty & Health

Life on Assistance – It's a circus. A couple of us on IA have been fortunate to be linked with caring and helpful financial aid workers. In several cases, however, treatment by workers administering programs and services has been demeaning, disrespectful and dehumanizing:

- My life the last couple of years has been all about preparing for change and then recovering from change. You spend three days bracing yourself to go see somebody in the Ministry because you never know who's going to be in there, or what kind of mood they're going to be in, or how much shouting there's going to be. Then you go see somebody in the Ministry, get your cheque, and then go to the grocery store with everybody else who's also been to the Ministry. Nobody's in a good mood... I spend another three or four days in bed recovering from the experience.
- When I go into the social assistance office, I try and have a really good attitude. But I feel degraded. Everyone's depressed. The people that work there and the people that go in there... I've come out of there bawling... Four months ago, I got a red flag on my cheque, which says you've got to come in and straighten something out... She went through all my papers and finally found the information that was already there in my file. Then it got flagged again... They already had that information too. This month, it's flagged again and I don't know why. Each time I have to come in, I have to pay for the bus fare.
- It's very degrading. I feel like a poodle, on show in a circus ring. Granted I'm not as well groomed... You're treated like you're 4 years old and they send your rent direct. You don't have the privilege of your landlord not knowing... You have to fight to have it deposited into your bank account so you can have enough pride in being able to pay it yourself.
- The very same agencies that are there to help people are in fact oppressing people by making them go through one hoop after another. It's like going through a maze. You enter. You go in one way. Before you know it, you're lost and you can't get out.

> I have a friend who was on Welfare. She got hired [as] a 'social worker'. Her character and spirit withered within months. I could detect her beliefs changing... Her 'training' washed away the memory of her experience and she used language like "protecting the system from 'those' people. It is our money they are spending." I listened to her tell me of the people she sees on Welfare: "Women just spread their legs and get pregnant again and again simply to stay on the system." With this new attitude, she compared her new virtues to those of 'people on Welfare'; I asked her how long she had been on the system before she got hired. Her reply: "Seven years." She was laid off a year later.

2. Health Services

Some of us receive excellent treatment from our GPs and other health professionals. We expected that to be the case for most of us, but too many report i) problems finding a doctor, ii) difficulties with the doctors we do have, or iii) health care professionals who either don't understand the challenges we face or make assumptions they shouldn't. There are enough of these complaints to suggest that improvement is needed and that some of us are being harmed by the current situation.

Doctor availability. No doctors in the Cowichan Valley are taking new patients. There had been one doctor taking patients, but he was located in an area that most us cannot reach. Those of us without doctors are out of luck. Those of us who are unhappy with our doctors have no option but to keep them. This makes us almost as bad off as the ones without doctors, since we may not be seeking our doctor's help when we should.

Lack of understanding, sensitivity and respect. Of the women who are unhappy with their GPs, the chief reason given is the doctor's lack of respect and apparent failure to listen. Some doctors appear to assume that 'weakness' in the form of tears goes hand in hand with low intelligence. Questions are left unanswered or given a cursory reply.

Three women were assumed to be drug addicts when they arrived at Emergency for the treatment of pain or after a collapse.

In two cases, tests verified later that there had been no drugs in the women's systems. In the third case, testing was denied.

A woman who was overwrought, in pain, and suffering from grief, was assumed not to know what she was talking about. She'd been asking for help. No one was listening:

- I don't believe in taking all this shit that is being pumped into my body, and I've said that to my doctor so many times. It's like: 'You're just not hearing me, are you?'
- I don't have a doctor right now. I need one. My previous doctor would not lower my medication. It numbs my emotions. I was going into treatment. I wanted to feel the healing. I couldn't do that if the medication was keeping me at one level. We agreed it was better that I seek another doctor. She did not refer me to another doctor. There is no new doctor. There's a shortage of doctors. [With her doctor refusing to reduce the medication, this woman went completely off it; with no new doctor, her condition is not being monitored.]
- A doctor told me, 'You're fat; you need to get out and walk'. What she didn't ask, or didn't care about, was that it was the middle of monsoon season. I didn't own a coat because I was busy purchasing coats for my children... When I said, 'That's just not possible', she didn't ask Why? She said, 'Well, accept you're going to be fat and die'.
- I have arthritis... My doctor..., instead of dealing with my real problems, immediately wants to give me pills for depression.
- [Of her special needs child]: They did tests after tests after tests. They'd say: Why don't you have a house? Why don't you have a husband? Why don't you have money? Why don't you, why don't you, why don't you? Not: You're doing so well considering you're a single mom and trying your best; your son seems to be such a happy child.

Treating depression, not its cause. We understand that doctors may be facing their own dilemmas. They see their patients in pain and want to help. They know that the best cure is prevention, but the prevention in this case is not within their power to provide. Still, we must make this point.

We have often been diagnosed by our doctors as depressed. Most of us are. However, the typical response is to start us on antidepressants, which many of us don't want.

One woman who was put on antidepressants, also has a stress-related skin rash. She connects the dots, illustrating why those who design social policies and health care policies should be communicating with one another: "They're willing to spend $200 a month on a drug. I would far sooner see that $200 in my cupboard and my fridge. It would go a lot further. Consequently, if we weren't so poor, I wouldn't be so stressed. If I wasn't so stressed and had better nutrition, I wouldn't have this rash to begin with."

She also wouldn't be depressed.

Mental health services. A few storytellers have received favourable, even excellent, care from Cowichan Valley's mental health services. Others have had poor experiences, often in the past, but also presently. That, and the fact that we may come from traumatic beginnings, can impede our ability to ask for help. Some mental health professionals do not seem to recognize this, assuming that a person needing help is able to ask for it:

- I've tried to reach out to the local Mental Health unit. Each time the response has shown a lack of understanding... In one phone call, [I was] asked, 'What do you want to do?' I told her I couldn't decide, that making decisions became harder the more stressed I became. She just waited at the other end of the line, repeating her question. I hung up.
- I can't beg... I did all kinds of begging when I was growing up: Please don't hit me, please love me, please look at me as a person. Now I won't beg.

We understand that the situation is not clear cut. For one, there may be legal difficulties. Also, in the first case there is respect implied in the mental health professional asking the question. Nonetheless, it needs to be understood that mere presentation at the door or at the other end of a phone line may be all a woman in crisis can manage.

3. Food

Poverty means having little or no nutritious food. Our stories provide ample descriptions of the Welfare diet. Not having land on which to grow fresh produce is one barrier, but there are other, less obvious, challenges.

Getting it. Due to lack of donations and/or the demand on volunteer resources to keep up, organizations that distribute food to the needy have to make some tough decisions:

- The food bank wouldn't give me food because the kids aren't with me 40% of the time. They're with me 33-1/3% of the time. Well, how do I feed them for those ten days?
- You have to be up at 8 o'clock or else you're going to miss the food hampers. If you're sick on the day they give them out, you have to wait a week.
- I wish I got cheese but no one gives it out.
- [A woman living alone]: With every food bank that there is ... they don't give you high protein food unless you have children. You have to say you have kids to get milk."

Special diets. Some of us have special dietary needs. A couple developed those needs after we got on the system. One is affected by two secondary conditions: i) she has a note from an out-of-province doctor, but the Ministry insists she get a note from a local doctor; ii) she hasn't a doctor.

One woman became a diabetic while on the Welfare diet; others are gaining weight and fearing the development of diabetes. Those of us with special dietary needs can apply to the Ministry for a Nutritional Supplement. A doctor must sign a form attesting to the need. Even with a doctor's note, Welfare may not provide the supplement. Either way, the supplement is likely to be insufficient. Our diabetic receives $15 a month.

Another case is a woman with a severe skin condition. Welfare paid for her to go to an endocrinologist. The endocrinologist prescribed a special high-protein, low-carb diet. That is expensive. The woman was denied the supplement.

4. Transportation and Communications

Half of us don't have phones. Few of us have cars. The public transit system operates infrequently, within limited hours, and not on Sundays and holidays. IA no longer provides transit fare.

5. Additional Issues

Credit. Equity is the name of the game when it comes to getting credit. Experience, training, wisdom, etc. do not count. Without credit, we may not be able to get a car (to go to work), a business loan (to start our own business), a home (to keep ourselves and our children safe)... There have been acts of kindness. A small local grocery store, for example, gave one of us credit for food when no one else would. Such acts, especially when it comes to credit, are rare.

Getting accounts under our own name after a marital breakup can be tricky and involve service fees.

We face credit traps: "I run out of money all the time for groceries. Because of that, I've got into that payday loan cycle."

If we have the misfortune to lose our car, or other product or service, we may have to pay a cancellation fee. A case in point is ICBC's fee for the cancellation of car insurance. Also concerning car insurance, none of us have money to pay a full year upfront. This means we must pay monthly, which also means we pay more for our insurance than someone who has money in the bank. In 2001, the interest rate was 8%. This is why a couple of us who have cars can't drive them.

Discrimination and cultural issues. "We *lost our language* and every other culture is out there yakking their language — on public buses and on public streets... I used to be *so angry* when I heard another's voice in their own language... I still am. Then I have to be a Canadian citizen and you're telling me I have to know *French*?!?!"

We have experienced discrimination when dealing with teachers or landlords: "We turned to looking for a new place and everywhere we looked, I ran into people who were prejudiced or who had lots of attitude."

Legal representation. We have been left vulnerable to inept lawyers or to no legal representation at all, and to spouses who had more money for legal representation than we did. In one case, Social Services removed children to an ex-husband when the woman fell ill and found herself in hospital for surgery. She had poor legal representation and only now is getting assistance to get her kids back.

In another case, "I had no representation to retain 50% custody; once custody was reduced to 45%, maintenance enforcement dropped their application for child support."

Stigma. Many of us have seen our friends or family draw away, as if they were embarrassed or fearful of our poverty. Some seem to think it will infect them. Family members deliberately or unconsciously bury their heads in the sand. Guilt sometimes plays a role too:

Policies of Exclusion, Poverty & Health

- My dad said ... 'Well if you're sick, just rest' — yeah, well, I've got to go do my laundry in the bathtub, so I'll pass on that. My family are clueless and they don't want to know what it's like.
- My relationship with my son is not good. He is fearful I will ask for something
- I saw my dad recently for the first time in over a year. When I was leaving, he offered me $20. I told him, 'That's not why I wanted to see you.'

The Future – In an Ideal World...

At the end of our last story interview, we did a little exercise. We imagined a future that was better than today and then described what that future looked like. For some of us, this was hard to do at first, since the exercise required tapping into our reservoir of hope. Once started, though, we had fun with it. Of 18 women, all share at least two of these visions: [4]

Work. In our future, all of us, with the exception of one, will be working fulltime in a job or business that contributes a valuable service or product. This vision is driven not so much by our wanting a decent income, which of course we do, but by our desire to feel better about ourselves:

- Having a job is important to me because I like to do something meaningful everyday.
- I want to work. It gets me out, it gets me moving, it gets me income.
- Work is important to me — just having a place to go everyday and being able to say that I'm at least beginning to pay my way through society.

The one exception has worked since she was 14. She dreams of retiring comfortably and pursuing her art.

Land/Home. Eight of us envision owning land or our own home: "I'm very proud of my home when I have a home. I make it into a nice place to be. I need to make my home beautiful. I need a home to make beautiful."

---

[4] Three women who had written their own stories did not include a section on the future.

To help others. Our wanting to help others comes up consistently, not just in 'the future' section at the end of our stories, but implicitly throughout the rest.

We became part of this project because we wanted to see change, because we did not want others to go through what we have. "When I read the goals of the project, I thought: I can have my voice heard. I can work with other women who want to see the same changes happen, to give women their strength and their dignity back."

That is what we intend to do; that is what we are doing.

Please see our report, Phase 2 — The Recommendations.

Phase 2 - The Recommendations

This document is companion to our report Phase 1 — The Issues, which details the themes that featured dominantly in our stories. We urge anyone who has not read the Phase 1 report to do so before reading this document. The two reports were written as complements to one another and knowledge of the contents of the first is assumed.

As was done with the stories and the Phase 1 report, the following is written in the first person plural and the writer of the report is one of the storytellers. All quotations are taken directly from the women's recommendations.

Before we begin...

Some of us could not sustain the required momentum to remain as committed to the project through Phase 2 and the formulation of recommendations, as we had through Phase 1. It was not that we did not want to stay the course, for most of us had been particularly excited by this aspect of the project when we first signed up. For those whose lives are moving on, particularly the full-time students, well, they are moving on. For the remainder of us, many have lives of instability, as foretold in the previous report. Some have been or are in the throes of moving, others are engaged in legal battles, still others have increasing health problems. For all of us, it is a considerable and sometimes impossible feat to find time and energy to devote ourselves to anything beyond getting past today. Do not assume by this that the project - and particularly the storyteller group - does not have every woman's support. It does to the extent that each woman is able to give it.

Phase 1 required less of us, particularly of those who were interviewed rather than wrote their own stories. This does not imply that doing our stories was easy, regardless of the method. The challenges included finding the courage to overcome our fear, shame and embarrassment to reveal our lives to a stranger. More courage was needed to let our stories go, to expose them and so ourselves to the world. The process also took a naïve trust that our voices would finally be heard and that change would happen as a result. It takes energy to sustain that hope.

At last count, we still have a solid core of ten or so women, the so-called 'strong ones'. So-called, because depression lurks in our lives too and threatens to undermine our efforts. Writing this report, for instance, is utterly draining and I find it hard to keep going.

The following recommendations represent the collective and majority opinion of ten storytellers. We know that we speak on behalf of the rest, since the others' issues are our own. Further, all but two storytellers remain in regular touch and offer their support and faith in our ability to do this for them.

People do not live in a country. They live in neighbourhoods within communities. People also do not normally live in isolation, which suggests that poverty does not happen to individuals divorced of a contextual setting. As much as we, the storytellers, may take some of the blame for our present circumstances, we do not take it all. Others were complicit, either by overt action or inaction. This is where community and government must accept their roles.

What may surprise readers is that we see the solutions to poverty coming from the grassroots. We see them as coming from individuals in a community, starting with ourselves, coming together to make things better for all. By strengthening our communities and advocating for change from within these strengthened positions, we can influence government policy.

Our recommendations fall into three major groups, with some minor overlap. For this report we treat each group separately and in the order they appeared with the most frequency and urgency during our conversations with one another. We approach each group in light of answering a single question:

R1. What can WE do now to help our neighbours understand the nature and existence of poverty in our community?

R2. What can WE AND OUR NEIGHBOURS do now to eliminate poverty in our community?

R3. What can GOVERNMENTS do now to prevent poverty from happening in Canadian communities in the future?

Raising public awareness and understanding of poverty is our most urgent need. By 'public', we mean especially our friends and families, co-workers, doctors, neighbours, grocers, and other people with whom we may come in contact regularly. Their transformed attitudes will go a long way to our feeling less marginalized.

The irony is that this group of recommendations requires us to take the lead and our lack of money will hamper our efforts. That will not deter us, however. As we show in the following, women in poverty can take effective action. We just have to find alternate ways of getting our message out.

The second group of recommendations prescribe further actions on our part and hinge on the success of our carrying out the first set of recommendations. In having raised community awareness and understanding, we will no longer be alone, but will have the support and encouragement of our neighbours and will be working alongside them.

For the third set of recommendations, we change focus, suggesting ways in which government can and should be involved in preventing poverty. We list this set of recommendations last because we consider it the least urgent of the three. Notice also that while the first two sets of recommendations prescribe actions that we must take to see any change come about, the last group of recommendations are for government alone. Cynics that we are, we do not believe government will implement our recommendations anyway.

In summary, we see the cure for poverty resulting from grassroots activity, and the prevention of poverty being assisted by provincial and federal funding. The first depends on our willingness to expose ourselves to public scrutiny, and then to work through the second set of actions with our communities' support. We encourage all women in poverty in communities across Canada to follow these steps.

R1. Awareness and Understanding

To women living in poverty, how often in the past while has someone looked right through you?

Until people notice us and begin the process of understanding the nature of poverty in Canada, nothing will change. What happens next, therefore, depends on us, which is what this group of recommendations is all about. These are actions that WE, women in poverty, must take to get people in our communities to stop avoiding the problem and ignoring that we exist.

On the nature of poverty

What people need to know

Poverty costs. It costs not only ourselves and our families, it costs the communities in which we live. Poverty disables and it isolates. Poverty excludes. It virulently attacks health, which is a human, no less than an economic cost.

Unhealthy people demand more of our healthcare system: they have more heart disease, Type 2 diabetes, and other chronic diseases. They have higher incidents of suicide and substance abuse. As our stories illustrate, these conditions are seldom causes of our poverty. They result from our poverty.

Unhealthy people cannot function to their optimum, and sometimes they cannot function at all.

While our health due to poverty may prevent us from contributing to society to the extent that we would like, we need our communities to be open to letting us do what we can. Our health recovery may depend on it. Moreover, everyone will gain.

People must also accept that events leading to trauma are the leading cause of poverty for women. Most often these events involve some form of sexual or other abuse, typically begun in childhood. Then unanswered calls for help further the assault and leave the traumatized child or woman untreated. These events set the stage for future vulnerability, such as exposure to partners who also are abusive.

How to get the word out.

None of the following actions, which women in poverty must do themselves, will be easy. Lack of any money or resources impose multiple barriers. Such an irony, isn't it? The very thing we want to advocate against stands in the way of our advocating against it.

It may not be obvious to people with even a little bit of money what our added barriers are, but consider these questions: How might you communicate quickly with media people, potential funders or community partners without a phone? How might you meet with others (even fellow marginalized others), without the means to get to the meeting? How might you arrive at a politician's office in decent shape if you have walked miles in the rain without adequate clothing or footwear? How might you appear intelligent and put together when you're depressed, drenched and literally feeling faint with hunger?

Considering the barriers, one has to wonder how our storyteller group managed to do anything at all. We did, though, and we have only just begun. We suggest other women do the same. We propose that women in poverty in Canada's communities mobilize, galvanize and politicize to get the word out. Here are some suggestions how:

The Recommendations

<u>Mobilize</u>
Whether you are on the system, living on a pension, one of the working poor or a student — in other words no matter what your situation — if you live below the poverty line, we suggest you begin taking the following steps:

    a) bring together other women in similar circumstances and work with them to form a group,
    b) meet as a group regularly to build trust and confidence among the members,
    c) unite with other cells to form a larger group that represents all women in poverty in your community.

We detail each step below.

Form a group. If you collect Welfare, Disability or Employment Insurance, for example, the administration office likely requires you to report regularly. Even if you have not met other women on the system yet, those occasions are ideal for doing so. While you wait for your appointment with your worker, approach other women who are also waiting. Begin a conversation. Ask them if they would be interested in meeting regularly with you and a few other women who are facing the same struggles.

Students trying to manage below the poverty line will know others students in similar circumstances. Do the same thing. Form yourselves into group.

Self-employed and other working poor (euphemistically referred as 'the underemployed') may not be so easy to identify or reach. But if, for instance, you work in a part-time minimum-wage job at a major retailer, you will have lots of company among your fellow employees. A disproportionate number of the self-employed have very low incomes. If you are a self-employed woman yourself, you may have associates who also are self-employed. Whatever the case, spread the word and encourage those who respond to join you in forming a group.

Immigrant women may already have a connection through a local intercultural society, so we suggest you reach out to others at the events your organization runs.

If you are a Native woman, on or off Reserve, you will have no trouble finding other Native women who live in poverty. That is a sad and appalling fact in Canada. We urge you to also form a group.

If you live in low-income housing or in a low-income area, your most likely source for contacts will be your neighbours. Start with people you know. If you do not know anyone, start up a conversation at the local food bank or where you do your shopping. If you attend a church, approach the minister. He/she may be able to help. Remember that isolation is one of our greatest barriers, so you may need to work at reaching out to others.

The idea is to start small, seeking to connect with women who would be the easiest for you to reach, both physically (you live on the same block or Reserve, you are standing in the same lineup or are working in the same booth) and socially (you are both on Welfare, working part-time at a local retailer's, single mothers, students, and so you share a common struggle — the roots for a common purpose).

It is possible that your group will be a mix of women of various backgrounds and situations. No problem with that! The objective is to connect with other women in poverty, however you achieve that.

Once your group becomes known, there may be women in your community who have lived, but do not now live in poverty who would like to join your group. The decision to accept them as members should be discussed openly among the rest. You may find, as we did with our group, that you need to build a strong, tight bond among current members first. For us, the matter seemed to be about trust and especially, self-empowerment.

Meet regularly to build trust and confidence among group members. Once you have even three women in your group, set a schedule to meet regularly, at least twice a month.

Not everyone will be able to come to every meeting, and it may make sense to vary the options in your schedule. For example, you might set aside 1pm on the 1st and 3rd Sunday of every month and 10am for the 2nd and 4th Wednesday. Women who are particularly keen may attend all four meetings, which would be great.

Here are some activities your group might start with:

1. Find someone to help you write your stories. You may find this most effective if the person is from the group, rather than an outsider.

Our group found the process of storytelling, although difficult, incredibly validating and empowering, which is why we recommend it. Beyond that, getting your story out and on paper, even if only you and the person assisting you ever see it, helps to bond the

The Recommendations

group and quickly establish trust. Why? Because each of you will have gone through that same 'trial by fire', which suggests a strong personal commitment to the cause.

2. Knowledge is a basis of power, so find out the government regulations and policies that govern the programs that members of your group are accessing. For example, if you are on BC Benefits, ask someone in your group who has Internet access to look up, download and print the BC Employment and Assistance Act.[5] This will help you determine your rights and obligations under the program.

This is important. Many in our group who are on the system were left in the dark about benefits they could have accessed. They were given either no information or disinformation.

3. Get rid of the shame. If we cannot do this, how can we expect others not to see us as shameful creatures? The *conditions* that allow poverty to exist are shameful, but poor women, simply in virtue of living in poverty, have nothing to feel shame about.

Ridding yourselves of the shame means no longer trying to hide your poverty. For mothers with children at home, that can be a particular challenge. Many mothers try to protect their children from the knowledge that they are poor, by developing highly convoluted energy-draining techniques for hiding the obvious. But kids know, and we think that trying to hide your family's poverty sends the wrong message. Why not be frank with your children and teach them, as one of our storytellers' parents did, that "it's OK to be poor; it's who you are that counts."

4. Stop the self-recriminations. Ditto the above. If we do not stop blaming ourselves and thinking 'if only I had...', how can we expect others to stop blaming us for our situation? Self-blame, together with harbouring shame, serve us nothing but further harm.

Incidentally, the storytelling process in Step 1 will go some way to helping members of your group feel better about themselves. You will discover that, while each woman is unique, you share many experiences in common, which suggests that the experiences have an external cause. In other words, it's not you!

5. Do an inventory of your groups' skills and abilities. This will help you work from a position of strength. We all have talents and hidden abilities. Find out what the members of your group have to offer. This is not just an aimless or 'feel-good' exercise, although you will feel a great boost after this is done. The inventory will be used

---

[5] Try www.qp.gov.bc.ca/statreg/reg/E/263_2002.htm

as a resource for carrying out the actions listed in our R2 group of recommendations.

Do not be surprised if you find the task of doing an inventory of your skills to be challenging. Many in our group did not know what their strengths and skills were. There can be good reasons for this, such as childhood abuse causing long-term identity problems. Then poverty itself helps erode identity. With people's sole focus being on surviving each day, they have neither the energy nor the money to develop or explore their abilities and interests. Therefore, do not expect to get this inventory task completed easily or quickly, although you may be lucky. It may require time and the assistance of all group members for women among you to uncover the talents hidden within them.

Unite with other cells to form a larger group representing all women in poverty in your community. This is the third and final step in becoming a force to contend with. By this time, you have formed a cell of anywhere from a half to a dozen or so determined and probably very angry women. Do not be disheartened if there are only a few of you. That is still a strong starting point.

Now begin reaching out to other groups. Do not merge your cell with the others you find. Keep your independence intact and continue meeting as you have, but at the same time begin seeking out and contacting student, senior, working poor, neighbourhood and other poverty groups.

If no other groups like yours exist in your community, seek out and encourage other women to form one.

As you seek out new groups, make certain that their members are people of the affected populations (not professionals working to represent such populations) and that the groups function democratically, informally and have a parallel, non-hierarchical structure. Hierarchical structures tend to exclude, set apart, and introduce a pecking order. Another reason for avoiding them is that we do not want more of the same. Instead, we want to show how things can be done differently, preferably without government bureaucratic interference and red tape. [6]

---

[6] Due to government policy, corporations, which registered charities and non-profit societies are, have no option but to have hierarchical structures.

The Recommendations

Galvanize

Now that your cell has connected with others to form a larger body, begin working as a united front to get your community's attention and interest. The idea is to galvanize your community into becoming politically interested and initiating other supportive actions to eliminate poverty in the area.

The first step, which is getting your community's attention, involves making yourselves visible and speaking out publicly. Having stopped or reduced the self-blame, the feelings of shame, and pretending you are not poor when you are, it is time to collectively force yourselves out into the open. We say 'force' because the community may be resistant.

We urge you not to think harshly of your community if its members exhibit this head-in-the-sand attitude. Many good-hearted people do not want to see a problem because they feel helpless to do anything about it. They need your help to understand that recognizing the problem, which first means recognizing you, is the first step toward a cure. Until you get the attention of your community, you will have to adopt the attitude of "We will not go away and we will not shut up."

1. Arrange to speak at local schools, city or regional councils, clubs and other organizations, including social service and business groups.

We suggest that you do these presentations in teams of two or three. This not only conveys a united front, but provides support to each presenter. Also encourage, but do not push, all group members to participate in these presentations. Some women may be too shy or not far enough along their journey to recovery and yet be excellent support workers behind the scenes.

2. Contact your local newspaper. Request that it run a regular 'Day in the life' column on poverty, written by people in poverty. The point is to help the public understand what not having money means for someone living in a Canadian community, to help them see that it restricts choice every day for having or doing the things that they take for granted.

3. If you cannot get your local paper to run a column or even if you can, create your own newsletter and distribute it around town. (Yeah, we know — money again. There may be some inventive ways around that; contact us if you need help.)

4. Because sexual and other forms of abuse in childhood make a woman vulnerable to future poverty, make this a key topic in

speaking engagements and in other communications, such as your newsletter. Include in the discussion that a) poverty itself is disabling and can be abusive, b) all of us, including ourselves, must stop blaming the victim and c) survivors of abuse who live in poverty can lose any recovery they previously gained.

Some people in your community will not care about the human cost of poverty. To win them over, show them the economic costs of keeping women such as ourselves in poverty — you might begin with your inventory of skills and abilities, or point to the economic values of having children raised to be strong, healthy and caring individuals. In other words, if you cannot win over corporate types by appealing to their compassion, strike where their passion is, their bank accounts.

5. Remember that gender discrimination and pressures to conform — not necessarily the same thing — were the #2 long-term predictors for (our) women's future poverty. Externally-imposed limitations can squash creativity, deny or challenge independent thought and enterprising efforts and stand in the way of personal fulfillment.

Make these issues known through your various communications efforts. As parents or guardians of young people, teach them to respect one another on all levels, and do this no less by example. Show that you value equally the talents, strengths, intelligence and coping skills of both sexes and each child. Encourage individuality. Do not concern yourself about non-conformist behaviour, unless it is illegal or hurting someone.

Again, if you cannot reach people by appealing to their compassion, use reason to show the economic costs of discrimination and pressures to do and be like everyone else.

The costs of the latter are not clear to many people. We are not saying that conformity itself is bad. After all, we do not want people driving on the wrong side of the road! What we are saying is that if society does not do more to celebrate diversity, it risks stifling or losing the creativity and inventiveness of those among us who think a bit differently. This can hurt society's prospects for invention and outside-the-box solutions to its problems.

Along similar lines and for similar reasons, we should promote the continued striving toward gender equality, emphasizing to the public that this benefits everyone.

The Recommendations

6. Speak, and/or write in your newspaper column, on behalf of local organizations that supply food to low-income people. Support their message that nutritious food is desperately needed, especially food with high protein content.

> *You have managed to get the attention of your community. That's HUGE – congratulations! The next step toward galvanizing your neighbours is getting their interest.*

1. Let your community know that its support is necessary for the healing process. The recovery from poverty should be a community-owned process that touches everyone and keeps us all accountable. When a community takes responsibility for, and works toward correcting its social failures, everyone gets to share in its success.

2. Inclusiveness is key to addressing poverty and marginalization. Inclusiveness means everyone is able to get to the places they need to go. It means everyone has access to the services they need, and the opportunity to participate in community events, sports and recreation. Inclusiveness means no one is forced by economic or physical circumstances to live in isolation. An inclusive approach is primary and crucial to ensuring that your community prospers to the benefit of all its members.

Inclusiveness is related to what we value. Once upon a time, goods were valued in light of the quality of their materials and construction (workmanship). Services were valued by the quality of their results (again workmanship). Then a dollar amount was applied to both and money morphed into a value all its own. The result was that the acquisition of money or 'assets' became the goal. Now it is the size of your bank balance or the extent of your credit that is the measure of your worth.

This situation must change. Help your community become more inclusive by emphasizing that it value people, not money, as its most important resource.

Also related to inclusiveness is the recognition of everyone's right to provide input. We therefore suggest that you consult with community leaders and organizations to determine methods for including everyone in discussions related to changes to, or the implementation of new services, development and infrastructure.

To achieve inclusiveness, communities will face some challenges. Not least of these will be the suspicion and distrust of the marginalized groups they are now trying to include. This suspicion is understandable. People long marginalized distrust the motives of anyone they do not know. The question always lurks, 'What do you want?' It will take some convincing that you want nothing more than to recognize and include them.

3. In the bad times. Emphasize the need for early intervention and community support for incidents of sexual and other abuse, family break-up, natural death or suicide. Get your community to realize that simple old-fashioned neighbourliness — keeping in contact with the people living next door, monitoring children at play, *just being friendly and caring for one another* — can go a long way to preventing problems.

Make it known that when questions of abuse do arise, your community must act quickly. It must *always believe the child* until there is proof otherwise. This does not mean that without evidence police should arrest an alleged offender. It does mean that immediate steps should be taken to protect the child.

<u>Politicize</u>

Having got the interest and support from your community, at least in principle, now begin working together to make poverty the foreground issue on the political landscape.

1. Become aware and act. Learn about the candidates in all elections, including municipal, select a candidate and vote.

2. Promote your political ideals through action. In all elections — municipal, provincial, federal — be vocal about your support. Become a member of a provincial and federal party (negotiate the membership fee). During an election, help with your candidate's campaign, but also be there for your party during off-election periods.

3. Do it yourself. Enter politics, beginning at the community level.

4. Get other women to vote. With the help of your community, determine a way of supporting the education and process necessary to get women to register and vote.

The Recommendations

> By now, your group has become a force to contend with. You have mobilized yourselves, galvanized your community and politicized the issues. You have made poverty visible and shown that alleviating the conditions that make it possible will benefit all members in your community.
>
> With community support behind you, things are getting exciting, because next you are going to

revolutionize...

R2. Community-Based Action

In this section, we suggest some very, and some not so very novel ideas. They involve rethinking the market economy and exploring alternatives, such as:

i. gifting
ii. moneyless exchanges of services and goods
iii. co-operative enterprises that serve transportation, grocery, housing, employment, childcare and other needs

There are several good reasons for women in poverty to start thinking and acting along these lines. First, all these initiatives, which we have ordered according to our preferences, support environmentally sound and sustainable practices. Second, in acting according to these principles, we passively resist the status quo. We so much as say: Society should function for the betterment of all. It isn't doing that. We know a better way. Follow us.

Gift economy

Generosity and caring among people in poverty is nothing new. If you have compassion, you do not want others to suffer as you do. You therefore give, even when that means having less or going without. You do it with no thought about getting anything in return.

We have seen this happen frequently in our own group. Women will share their small supply of food so that others go less hungry. They share their 'wealth' to alleviate another woman's even heavier burden. They pass along a gift, one given to them by a family member, because they want to soothe another's heart and that item is all they have. Above all, they give their encouragement and support.

Gifting is a fine principle for doing more than just sharing in bad times or for celebrating holidays and special events. It could be the start of a major revolution. Indeed, we suggest that gifting should not be left for 'special' at all, but be our guiding principle for day-to-day life. We would like to see it replace the present market economy.[7]

What is a *gift economy* and what would it mean to live by its principles? This is easiest to explain in terms of comparison between the two systems. In a market economy, exchange is the practice and profit is the goal. The guiding question in a market economy is, 'How much can I save or profit by this transaction?' With profit as goal, there is always a winner and a loser: I have saved at cost to you, or you have profited at cost to me.

With gift economies, the guiding question is, 'What do you need and is there a way I can help?' Note the phrasing of the last. It is not part of the gifting philosophy that people give what they cannot. The assumption is only that people give to the extent that they can.

In gift economies, there is no 'What's in it for me?' The focus turns outward toward friends, family, neighbourhood and community. This explains why communities with a gift economy have far fewer problems with inequality, belonging and inclusiveness.

The key concern that most people have about gift economies are the takers, those individuals who will not give anywhere near what they can. Aboriginal cultures based on a gift economy typically use ostracism as their sanction of choice. Ostracism bases its effectiveness on the sense of belonging and closeness to community that grows in each child from birth. In cultures based on caring for one another, to be ostracized can be devastating.

Even though a market economy surrounds us and we cannot avoid our own psyches being steeped in it, some ways do exist for us to begin building a pocket gift economy. The key, so that the market economy does not take advantage of us, is to keep our gift economy closed to non-participants. As people in your community learn what you are doing, more are likely to want to participate.

---

[7] In North America, the promotion of a gift economy has largely been driven by Genevieve Vaughan. First credit, however, goes to the many aboriginal cultures of the world, whose very survival has depended on the principle of giving. One excellent Canadian source is Jeannette Armstrong, of the Okanagan Nation.

The Recommendations

The following lists 26 ideas for getting started and includes practices that most people do already. We include the latter to emphasize that gifting is already present in our lives and that the suggestion is only to extend the principle beyond those practices.

- Give a smile or a hug.
- Share a meal with someone who is hungry or lonely.
- Offer a ride to someone who has no car.
- Get to know your neighbours. Offer help when needed.
- Share your knowledge.
- Give someone a neck and shoulder massage.
- Share your garden with someone who hasn't one.
- Read a story to a child or elderly person who cannot see.
- Hem a skirt or patch a knee for someone who cannot sew.
- Shop for someone who cannot get around.
- Become a Big Sister.
- Give away clothing you no longer wear.
- Give (not loan) money to someone who needs it.
- Do baby-sitting or childcare for free.
- Write a letter for someone who cannot write.
- Teach someone to read.
- Be company for someone who is isolated.
- Reach out to people who are marginalized; listen and observe.
- Bake a loaf of bread or pick flowers from your garden. Give them to a friend or neighbour.
- Use open-source software, encourage others to do the same and offer tutorials.
- Offer free school tutoring.
- Collect and repair old bicycles from the neighbourhood. Leave them in various locations for free use by all.
- Share your home with someone who hasn't one.
- Share laughter and tears with someone who is alone.
- Never, ever pass someone by in the street without looking them in the eye and acknowledging them.
- Do research on gift economies and spread the word!

We are not naïve enough to think we will convince any dyed-in-the-wool capitalist or corporate executive that transitioning to a gift economy is a good idea, but that will not deter us. Besides, since we literally have nothing to lose, why not try starting something new?

Also, we do not imagine going from start to finish in one easy step. Rather, the achievement of our goal — a full-fledged gift economy — will not happen without working first through our other

two community based alternatives: co-operatives and exchanges. The market economy would otherwise eat us up, taking advantage of our gifting philosophy (aka 'gullibility') and leave us no further ahead.

Moneyless Exchanges

The guiding principle with moneyless exchanges is to give in order to get. We therefore do not consider them as ideal a solution as gift economies. However, exchanges are less profit-oriented than money-based systems, which makes them a good first runner-up to a gift economy. They also trade in the same goods and services that are provided free in a gift economy, as you can see from this sample list:

- Establish a community closet – donate clothes you no longer wear in exchange for others.
- Promote and participate in the local community kitchens program. You get to take home super low-cost meals!
- Promote and participate in the local community gardens program. You get to take home fresh produce.
- Trade services:
    - Do you sew? Do alterations in exchange for a ride.
    - Can you cut hair? Do haircuts in exchange for food.
    - Are you a computer hardware or software expert? Offer tech assistance in exchange for ___ .
    - Do you do carpentry, plumbing, electrical work, ...?
- Share your knowledge in exchange for others sharing their knowledge with you.

Communities using exchanges on a larger scale sometimes create their own currency to track the trade of goods and services. Saltspring Island (off Vancouver Island, on the westernmost point of Canada) had Saltspring Dollars once upon a time. We do not know if they still do. Ithaca, New York uses hours as its basis of valuation, similar to exchanges based on time dollars.

We do not see the advantage of exchanges where a new currency or valuation system replaces another. The underlying theme remains: What is owed to whom and how much?

The Recommendations

Co-operative enterprises

Co-operatives have been around for a long time in Canada and are growing in popularity. That they can function well within market economies makes them ideal starting points toward a gift economy.

Almost all co-ops require seed money and material resources, so you will not be able to start one up without funding support. Assuming your success with our first group of recommended actions, you will have gained your community's support. Hopefully, that comes with financial backing. You might also be fortunate to receive government funding (see the R3 group of recommendations).

Whatever services are needed, co-ops can provide them:

- Childcare. A childcare co-op need not require money to get started. In its simplest form, a group of parents is formed and members exchange childcare services.
- Employment. Members create an enterprise that markets goods or services. The co-op is owned by the employees. A spin on this concept is to include workshare.
- Food. There are several variations of food co-ops. In its simplest form, each person contributes what s/he can for food. Then a delegation of members goes shopping for items that can be bought in bulk. (Necessitates a vehicle to cart the goodies home.)
- Housing. These co-ops are usually single developments containing multiple dwellings. Members share the costs or labour for maintaining the common areas.

   We prefer cohousing to housing co-ops. Cohousing neighbourhoods combine the autonomy of private dwellings with the advantages of shared resources and community living. For more information, refer to the website of The Canadian Cohousing Network: www.cohousing.ca.
- Transportation. Essentially a car pool, transportation co-ops can have anywhere from one to a dozen vehicles of different types. If you start without vehicles, access to funding will be a major obstacle.

Many more types of co-ops exist. Some provide services only to members and money is not traded; they function much like exchanges. Other co-ops are full-fledged enterprises that serve the wider market and benefit co-op members through profit (e.g., credit unions).

R3. The Role of Government

As readers will have picked up by now, we have little regard for provincial or federal government interventions. We think governments should get out of the social service business. They are terrible at it. In many cases, the programs governments design and run do more to exclude and marginalize people than any condition they are designed to address.

Rather than run social service programs, governments should fund community-based groups and organizations to manage, determine the needs for and design social programs for their communities. Community- and volunteer-based groups could manage the tasks far more effectively and cost-efficiently than government.

With our take on governments' efforts to deal with social issues, do we see them having any role, other than as funders of community-based programs? Yes. The federal government should ensure universality of livable economic conditions throughout Canada and our aboriginal communities, and the provincial, territorial and regional governments should fund and otherwise support the programs that communities determine will promote social inclusion.

To governments, we make the following recommendations.

1. Guaranteed Annual Income for All (GAIA)

No surprise here. Workers in the field have been advocating for a guaranteed income for decades, and finally one provincial government is seriously looking at the idea (Quebec).

To clarify, we advocate for a basic livable income for every man, woman and child in the country. At income tax time, the amount would be adjusted per household according to the number of persons and dependents in that household, and it would be regained, in full or in part, from households not needing it.

Most groups advocating for a GAIA suggest the amount be equal to the Low Income Cut Offs (LICOs). Since no government is likely to agree to that, we suggest the amount be set at the LICOs, plus 50% of the poverty gap.[8]

---

[8] This is the difference between the poverty line and the average income of households below the line. For example, suppose the current year LICO for a single person household in a small urban area is

While a GAIA may seem an expensive proposition, in the long run it will save money. Not at first, of course, because we will have to pay off all those laid-off Welfare, Old Age Security and other social service workers. They would have one consolation, however. Should they not find work before their payouts run out, they need never fear the haunting spectre of homelessness. The GAIA will protect them. We could even use those old buildings for housing! (Are we being a tad satirical? Well, sure. Can YOU imagine any government doing something this reasonable?)

2. Funding Community-Based Employment and Training Programs

Communities can best identify what their citizens and neighbourhoods need in terms of employment assistance and training. Therefore, governments should provide no-strings-attached funding that goes directly to communities. The communities, in turn, would determine how those funds should be used.

This gives more power and responsibility to the people we elect to run our communities. This is a good thing. Our community officials are easier to reach, they live right where we live, and they are far more apt to listen to us than someone whose purpose is to attend to the interests of a broader landscape.

In terms of community-based programs, there is much talk these days about community economic development (CED). In its most recent form, CED places social inclusion at the forefront of its goals.[9] The words 'community economic development' imply something to do with skills and employment. It makes sense, therefore, that employment and training programs be conceived and developed from within community and as part of an overall CED plan.

Communities that accept the CED philosophy would ensure that all who needed access to their employment and training programs would be served, and they could identify and act on those needs more quickly than upper-level governments.

$12,500 and the average income of such households is $7,000. The poverty gap is the difference between the two: $5,500.
[9] See, e.g., *A Literature Review on Social Inclusion and CED*, Michael Toye and Jennifer Infanti. The Canadian CED Network, 2004. Downloadable from the CCEDNet website: www.ccednet-rcdec.ca.

3. Frontline Personnel – Awareness Training

This section applies to all levels of government, non-governmental organizations and to all professionals who provide community service, regardless of who funds that service.

We urge sensitivity and awareness training to all frontline social services workers, police, medical and other institutional personnel on the real issues facing women struggling alone or raising children in poverty.

Among the things of which professionals need to be much more aware are that:

- women in poverty are masters of the cover-up. Do not assume when we talk or look presentable that we are doing better financially, or that we haven't a disability (you can be sure we're clinically depressed), or that we have means to get around, or...
- just about any assumption you make about us will be wrong.
- it is unwise to assume that
   - we lack intelligence because we cry.
   - we are fat/thin by choice,
   - our clothes are threadbare because we don't care
   - we are drenched because we simply 'got caught in the rain' (we probably walked miles to see you), or....

Everyone needs to know this, but especially professional people whose jobs are more likely to place them in contact with women in poverty.

Assuming government does not make good on the above advice, we make the following alternative recommendations:

1. Changes to Welfare

i. Have the entry process begin with applicants seeing Registered Nurses, whose purpose is to spot health problems related to poverty and to advocate on the applicants' behalf. The process should not begin with social workers trained as financial aid consultants, as though applicants' lack of budgeting skills are the cause of their poverty. That's insulting and untrue in almost every case.

The Recommendations

ii. Allow social assistance recipients to keep their savings. Do not make poor people poorer by forcing them to cash in RRSPs, RESPs, and other savings before they are eligible for social assistance.

iii. Institute mandatory professionalism that respects and honours individuals going through the process of poverty. We suggest mediation training, which would ensure that the person who wants this vocation is able to empathize with the circumstances facing people in poverty.

iv. Change how social service personnel refer to the people they serve. When talking to, or referring to Welfare recipients in their presence, call them by name — not by first name, but as 'Ms.', 'Miss', or 'Mrs.'. Do not refer to them as 'the client'.

v. Increase support payments to a realistic level to meet basic shelter and nutritional needs.

vi. Make the system user-friendly, open and transparent. Ensure full written and verbal disclosure to all new applicants of their rights and Welfare policies. In British Columbia, provide them with the latest copy of the BC Employment & Assistance Act and go over it with them. In other provinces, do similarly.

vii. Allow supports to families at least comparable to foster care.

viii. Include realistic support to people who are disabled and families with special needs children.

2. Education & Training, Access to Programs

i. Make access to government employment-related programs — education and training, loans for entrepreneurs, resume assistance — user-friendly and available to a wider base of people, not only to persons on the system. This will prevent individuals and their families from reaching the depths of poverty.

ii. Allow people on the system to study for university degrees. Since a Bachelor's Degree is increasingly demanded of employment applicants, offering people on low income more 'Joe job training' will not serve them long-term.

iii. Diversify the types of programs and financial aid offered and by whom. Do not allow one organization to monopolize in these areas, which is currently the case with Cowichan Valley's FutureCorp and its self-employment training and assistance programs.

The programs run by Community Futures Development Corporations are intended by government to be community-based. One of the reasons these efforts do not succeed to the extent they could is that the community does not design these programs or their related policy. For example, eligibility of applicants is specified at the centres of government, not locally.

3. Food Security

i. People lacking in nutrition ultimately cost our healthcare system. We prefer to see money spent on prevention rather than on interventions to fix an avoidable problem. We therefore strongly recommend that universal access to nutritious food be included as a right in the Canada Health Act and that this right be recognized in all other relevant legislation.
ii. Increase Welfare support allowances to accord with i.

4. Health

Because income and social inclusion are top social determinants of health, apply health promotion principles when designing economic and social policy:

i. Before any policy is revamped or new policy drafted, do a complete Health Impact Assessment.
ii. Ensure that the people writing policy sit at the same table with an equal number of professionals in the Social Determinants of Health field and representatives of the population(s) of people likely to be affected by the policy.
iii. Do not focus money on healthcare at the expense of health promotion programs. Seriously addressing the social determinants of health, such as income, housing and social inclusion will reduce the demands on healthcare services.
iv. Promote recognition that poverty in a woman's life can signal recent or childhood events of a sort causing severe trauma; also that the woman may never have been treated and charges, if applicable, never been pursued.
v. Ensure more training and services for parenting, family counselling and support of those who experience abuse and sudden death.
vi. Provide extended healthcare and basic dental coverage to reduce pharmaceutical use. Ensure coverage includes treatments by clinical psychologists (not just psychiatrists), naturopathic physicians, physiotherapists, occupational and massage

therapists, chiropractors and other professionals. Implement coverage for alternative health services (homeopathy, eldercare, counselling). Recognize that optometry and dental care are basic health needs.
vii. Ensure full prescription coverage for anyone below the LICOs. Include coverage of herbal remedies prescribed by naturopathic physicians.

5. Volunteerism & Unpaid Work

Money has become a value where it once represented a value. The cost has been the devaluation of labour. If one gets paid for what one does, that work is deemed worthwhile. If one does not get paid, one's work is inferred to be inconsequential. This means, for example, that a woman on social assistance who volunteers at the local food bank, Big Sisters organization and is a peer counsellor is considered — as she scrambles around doing all these activities — to be a laggard and doing nothing worthwhile.

In similar fashion, non-profit organizations are deemed more or less worthy in virtue of their annual operating budgets. The social services they provide, because they are *social* services, are often seen by government and the corporate world as non-essential services. That at least is the perception because of the emphasis on money. We therefore make the following recommendations:

i. Value unpaid work. Count hours spent on unpaid work (childcare, eldercare, community or charitable deeds) and give tax credits accordingly.
ii. Grant charitable-tax status to organizations working on advocacy and fund core, not just project needs. Governments increasingly depend on non-profit societies and registered charities to provide social services, yet these organizations are seriously under funded. Most are in crisis, having to deal with fewer volunteers, added government regulations, and less money and resources.

6. Transportation

i. Improve public transportation, making it accessible and available to all 24/7.
ii. Make public transportation passes available free to all households below the LICOs.

7. Communications

Make basic phone service free to all households below the LICOs.

8. Housing & Utilities

i. Rather than building more subsidized and low-income housing complexes, create a housing subsidy similar to the BC Government's SAFER program. SAFER (Supplementary Aid for Elderly Renters) is currently available only to single-person households whose occupants are 60 years of age or older. There are at least two good reasons why this program should be extended to all households falling below the LICOs.

First, housing subsidies are portable and allow eligible households to go into the private sphere where housing stock meets basic security and sanitation needs.

Second, subsidizing renters (not rental units, where payment is made to the landlords) promotes sustainable economically mixed communities and enables members of low-income households to see a different reality from their own. Low-income housing can amount to nothing more than ghettos, giving people in them the view that no other possibilities exist but hunger, addiction, violence and early death.

ii. Allow the subsidy mentioned in (i) to be applied to mortgage payments, not just to rental payments.
iii. Make basic utilities free to households under the LICOs and provide assistance to pay for their heating fuel. Also encourage through financial aid the use of alternative fuel options.

9. Legal Representation

i. Reinstate complete services under Legal Aid.
ii. Ensure that an advocate is assigned to represent children of families going through divorce.
iii. Tighten up child maintenance procedures to ensure basic needs are covered.

10. Daycare

We advocate universal daycare. At the least, governments should increase daycare funding and availability.

11. Credit

Devise a mechanism for enabling women in poverty to acquire credit. We think this is best handled at the community level, assisted with upper-level government funding, perhaps through the Status of Women.

We hope that our recommendations will be considered seriously and that at least some of them will be adopted. We particularly hope that other women in poverty will start on the path of mobilizing, galvanizing and politicizing in their communities. To those women, we say:

Good luck and contact us if you need help.